THE GOSPEL ACCORDING TO ISSA

An account of scripture as depicted by a
dog named Issa

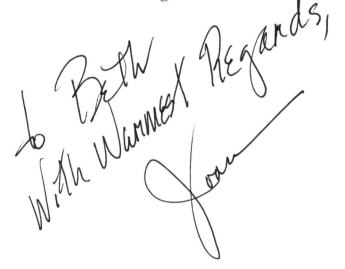

To Beth
With Warmest Regards,
Joan

Joan Black

Oct 2013

The Gospel According to Issa

Cataloging-in Publication data

Black, Joan

The Gospel According to Issa

1. Bible Characters—Fiction 2. Jesus Christ—Fiction 3. Jesus—Friends and

associates--Fiction

ISBN-13: 978-1482634624
ISBN-10: 1482634627

Table of Contents

Dedication

My twin sister, Jean, who introduced me to dog love.

This book is also dedicated to our dogs that are now in heaven: Gracie, Thurber, Wren, Little Duke of Sun Down, Diablo, Chesai, Dewey,Blip, Bucky and P-Nut. And to the dogs that our still with us: Lenny, Roxie and Migo.

And to my wonderful companion, Rupert Augustine, who, despite being of the feline persuasion, inspires me daily.

"You think those dogs will not go to heaven! I tell you they will be there before any of us."
(Robert Louis Stevenson)

CHAPTER 1

One summer's day I observed my master to be lost in thought. He didn't seem much interested in playing chase or rubbing my head, like he usually loved to do.

I am a mixed breed dog. A mutt is how many would describe me. I am part Canaan dog, on my Jewish side. My father was a Jew. My mother was a Ibizan hound born and bred in Jericho, outside of the big Jerusalem city. She was not Jewish, but a Palestine dog.

My mother, Madee, had my two sisters and me some weeks before we were supposed to be born. It was a rainy day, and we were in the hills around Jerusalem when she went into labor. My father, Jacob, was tending to a lamb that had wandered from the herd. My mother ended up having the three of us in a cave.
She stayed there with us in the cave until we were old enough to move into the small town of Jericho. The Jericho masters who cared for my parents were very good and kind.

My sisters were very well behaved and never strayed far from home.

I, however, was not nearly as well behaved. One day when I was a young pup, I wandered some miles from my home. I ended up lost, in the hills around my home and got into a very troubling mess.

I fell into a steep crevice and found myself very stuck. To my great relief, I was rescued by a young man who heard my cries. He had been wandering in the hills just like me. When he saw me stuck, he spoke to me.

I was so scared. He told me to be calm, and I obeyed.

He lowered his girdle, which he looped in a fashion that secured my front legs. Up I came. It was as if the mountain parted just for me. I was to be forever in his debt. I still have a little limp from the accident, but never minded it much considering the grim alternative.

The young man who rescued me was a Jew. His name was Jesus, Jesus of Nazareth. And on that day, my life changed forever. I followed him home and vowed never to leave his side.

But Jesus wanted to make sure my parents wouldn't be worried. So he took me back home to Jericho. My parents were very happy to see me safe. Jesus asked my parents if he could adopt me.

It was obvious to everyone that this young man and I needed to be together. So on that day I kissed my family goodbye and promised to visit them often, which I did.

And so it went that I moved into the home of Jesus and his parents Mary and Joseph in Nazareth.

*****

But as I was saying, on that summer day when my master was lost in thought, I began to worry.

He was studying maps and reading a pile of books. He was having me look at the pictures of distant lands and talking about travel and adventure. He read many of the books aloud to me and asked me what I thought. It was interesting, these ideas and philosophies, but I was content with the hills and my master and my homeland. No need for much of anything else for me.

He was just past his youth. A young adult I suppose and I was just approaching my second full year. Despite his youth, many people in our community spoke of my master's wisdom and knowledge. Even the rabbis were astonished at his grasp of scripture and interpretations. He could read and write like a wise man. And, he was kind and loving beyond measure. I was honored to be his animal.

He was wise, but he was also curious. He studied maps and knew of other worlds. He wanted to speak and listen to other wise men and teachers. He had heard of prophets and holy people who lived in the East.

Due to this curiosity, we began to wander around to another side of the mountain more and more. From our new viewpoint we could look onto a stretch of desert as far as the eye could see. We sat for hours and looked at the caravans passing by, always going eastward.

One day he said to me, "I would love to travel east."

My heart sank. I had heard many stories about how many men and many dogs never returned home from this faraway Orient land. They ate dogs and were heathens who might just boil my master in a pot of onions and carrots. I had heard of such horrors.

My master, Jesus, had heard other kinds of stories. His mother Mary had told him about the wise men from the East who came to visit him when he was born. They had followed a star to find him and they brought him precious gifts from these very faraway lands.

Mary still kept the oils of Frankincense and Myrrh and when she burned them, the notion of exotic and wondrous possibilities filled our house. My young master loved the fragrances and became quite determined to follow their distant call.

Master and I eventually moved in closer and closer to the caravans. So close, it was as if we had become a part of it. The camel bells rang so sweet across the desert. The spicy lentils cooking, the flat breads baking, the sweet incense burning. Even the honey dripping from clay jars smelled of desert flowers and enchantment. On one occasion, a Nomad from the caravan trail gave us a taste of the honey.

We went home late on these days. My master's father would say to us,

"Beware of the Nomads. They can be dangerous."

One day, as we watched a caravan pass, a few of the Nomadics sat with us and told us about the great lands and adventures that lay ahead. They told my master that when the full moon showed in the sky above Jerusalem, they would be setting out again. Then they asked my master to join them. "We will keep watch over you and promise your safe return. We will visit many lands through Kashmir and the Punjab, up into the Himalayas. Come. Come with us. You will have much to say to the Brahmins and they will listen to you. It is in the stars. It is written. They await you."

I was frightened for my young master. The desire for adventure and knowledge was great, and now, it seemed that it was destiny for my master to leave and speak to these holy men so far away.

Master please don't go, I wanted to say

Some days later he came to me and touched my ears. He told me that when the next full moon came over Jerusalem City, twenty-eight days away, he was going to go with the caravan people.

I begged him not to leave me. I begged him to let me join him. I told him I would protect him from all harm.

9

"You need to stay here and care for my Mother and Father. This trip is far too dangerous for a dog as young as you."

I begged; I rolled over; I caught a fish for him straight from the Sea of Galilee.

Nothing changed his mind.

As the twenty-eight days came near to an end, he fawned over me; he played with me, and patted my head and rubbed my belly and ears every day.

Then the night of the full moon arrived.

My master was up way before dawn. Mary and Joseph were still asleep. He packed his holy books and writing tablets.

He left a note:

My dear mother and father,
A journey is ahead for me, which has long since been
decided for me to make. You will see me on my return
and I can tell you, surely, this much I know.
Your son

He then turned to me and knelt beside me. He rubbed my ears and kissed my nose. He quietly shut the wooden door behind him, and he was gone.

I tried to hide my tears.

Near my bedside carpet he left me a note:

My dear friend, thank you for your devotion.
One day we will be together again.

My grief was an agony beyond measure.

The small fire was burning low on the morning that he left. I kept hearing him say: "No!" And as much as I wanted to follow him I stayed.

I must always obey my master.

I couldn't get up for some days. Mary and Joseph were grieving with me. I wasn't interested in food and hardly drank a drop of water. My best friend—my only friend, was gone. "Oh master I miss you so."

On the third night after his departure my bones couldn't be lifted from the floor. My dog soul...my dog heart were broken. I fretted into a sad sleep.

I dreamed of the caravan. I saw my master with the nomads. I knew through my dream and the look in my master's eyes, that he did miss me.

When I woke up I was thoroughly confused. I wanted to be obedient and yet I felt that it was my duty to follow him.

On the day after my dream, I woke up to Mary and Joseph making a fuss in the front room. A stray dog had followed Joseph home from his early morning walk. This dog was older than me. He was big and strong and seemed brave, like a soldier. When he saw me he wagged his tail and approached me. He said to me, "Go and follow your master. I am sent here to protect Mary and Joseph."

I licked his head and wagged my tail. My heart pounded with a joy so great I thought I would leap over the moon. The stray dog told me to go to Jericho and a dog named Ali would direct me from there.

The next day I set off for my great journey.

I ran to the house of Ali, the dog in Jericho. Ali told me to look for a greyhound named Romey and I would receive further instructions at the market. The market was full of fruit and copper pots; beautiful carpets, sea salt and fragrances that made me feel giddy.

A beautiful female dog named Romey met me at a merchant's table where all sorts of fresh mint and coconuts were being sold. She nudged me and we convened our meeting under her master's table of wares. She was so pretty. She told me to catch the caravan past Baghdad. She said the caravan was on its way to India and that they would cross through the Kashmir pass into the great country of India. "That is where they are headed: The Himalayas."

I started to run because I felt that the longer I was with Romey, the harder it would be for me to leave. She had brown eyes with lashes that melted my heart. I could tell she liked me too.

She was stronger than me and reminded me of my mission. "Issa. Follow this scent." She put a camel's tassel in front of my nose. And then she looped a silk ribbon though the tassel and tied it around my neck.

I started to run, for the temptation to stay with Romey was so strong. I thought if I stayed one more moment I would weaken and forgo my journey. I started to run, but before my feet made haste, she stopped me and said, "Issa, I met your master when they came though this way. He petted my sister who had been lame since birth. Now she runs with full speed. Your master is great and you must go to him. Good luck Issa."

We touched noses and I felt a tingle in my heart.

"Find him and be safe and maybe someday you will return to visit me again."

It was hard to leave her beauty and kindness behind, but I turned to the east and made my way fast across the desert toward my beloved master. I ran and ran through the nighttime sand, still warm from the scorching daytime sun. I learned that I could only travel at night in the safe light of the moon. I ran till my legs screamed for me to stop. I would rest in what shade I could find during the day. I found water in odd places along the way.

Sometimes in the larger cities, a lake or a riverbed would quench my thirst and provide a fish or two to eat. All the way on my journey towards Baghdad the kindness of men and the generosity of nature kept me strong and able. Until, that is, one night just outside of Baghdad.

I was so tired and I looked a fright. My fur was sandy and my tail was tangled with small burrs, my ears were covered with a clay type mud. And my limp, my childhood limp rendered me almost crippled. I was losing hope. Fear had replaced my joyous leaps. I felt tired and defeated. I was near Ar Ramadi not far from Baghdad.

In my weariness, I rested near a small desert pond. I picked up a smell. My camel tassel told me that the camels leading my master had been in this area some weeks earlier. Despite my aching bones and my footpads, broken and bloody from my travels, I was comforted, knowing that I was at least on the right path.

I had fallen into a sleepy state under the palm trees shadows when I suddenly felt a net cover me and ropes tighten around my front and back paws.

Then I saw them: A band of frightful thieves. They captured me and were determined to kill me, skin me and boil my bones for dinner. I was in a fine mess.

I thought of my master. I thought of my girlfriend, Romey. I thought of Mary and Joseph, and my heart sank.

I'm a dead dog.

*****

When the sun descended and the moon rose full, the thieves approached me. They were laughing and

14

discussing what a fine supper I would make. It was difficult to look into their faces. Their eyes were black and smeared with a coal pencil. They screamed with the pitch of a wild boar as they pinched and pulled on my neck and hind legs. One of the thieves grabbed my jaw and yanked my head nearly backwards. He looked at my teeth. "Ah yes, a fine necklace for me." Then he laughed so loud the ground shook beneath me.

They dragged me (I was still tangled in the silk net and my paws were tied up with rope) toward the campfire. A giant stew pot bubbled and boiled in front of me. I looked into the night sky and cried out to master, my dearest friend, "I think I've done it this time…. Help?"

From out of nowhere my master's voice spoke to me. His voice said,
"Dance Issa. Dance!"

Now my master had taught me many tricks and games. He taught me to roll over, to walk backwards, make a twirl in the air, dive into water, talk and dance!

From my netted jail I stood and began to dance for the thieves.

They looked at me dancing and began to move and sway to the rhythm of my movements. One of the thieves played an instrument with bellows. His music hummed loudly across the desert dunes. And then, sure enough, another thief started playing a Tabla drum. The rolls of the drum and the hums of the bellows and the nighttime breeze made for a complete intoxication of folly. The thieves began to clap and dance. Spinning and spinning. Spinning and spinning. Their purple and crimson skirts blowing and lifting like tops from a carnival show.

As I danced, the net began to tear. The rope around my front and back legs loosened. In their folly, for they were dizzy and falling all about, I was able to walk backwards and dance to my freedom. They had temporarily forgotten about having me for supper.

When I got past the tents at the camp's edge, I ran into the bad men's camels and mules. They were very suspicious of me, as they were trained to cry out to their masters if they spied an escaping prisoner. One of the head camels was about to turn me in. I noticed her nostrils flaring. She smelled my tassel. "Where did you get this tassel?"

I whispered to her, "A friend in Jericho tied it around my neck to help me catch up with my master's caravan."

This very tall camel looked deeply at me and smiled. She whispered to me, "My brother is with the group you are looking for. His name is Briden. They are far to the east, but you can catch them if you make haste. Go now and be safe. Tell my brother his sister Chamon blessed your escape from the scoundrel thieves."

I told her to come with me, but she was too weary to follow me east. I told her that maybe one day we could rescue her. With that, I thanked her and she let me pass unseen through her long legs.

I ran like lightening and did not look back until I was some far distance away, then I turned around. From where I looked at the edge of a desert cliff, I saw the glowing light from the thief's campfire. It was just a speck, yet over the vast starlit desert; I could hear them still clapping and making music and their shadows still spinning and spinning.

I was so grateful for my escape.

"Dance. Dance!" It was my master's voice so clear in my head. He saved me from sure death. And that night, when I knew I was safe from the bad men, I rested. I thanked my master for saving me and then I fell into a sweet slumber. I slept all the next day, and when the moon rose, I took out again.

Finally, I passed through Baghdad and was faced, once again, with a desert that stretched as far as the eye could see. The further east I went, the more staggering the mountains became. It was a struggle to make it up these treacherous passes. I asked some mountain goats along the way to guide me. I had a group of three stay with me until I made it to the Kashmir Pass.

I had become so ragged and rough that I wondered if my master or Romey or anyone from my past would even be able to recognize me.

The mountainous regions of this land were craggy and dangerous. On more that one occasion I would slide or fall and have to lay still for a day or two to recover and let my bones heal. My limp was getting worse and the terror of falling into a crevice put a fear in me so fierce that I just about gave up.

It occurred to me that I might never be able to catch up with my master. The more these incessant thoughts of doom and failure took over, the more I was unable to move. My muscles were giving way and a dread came over me. I was alone and sad. When I found a small cave to hide in I curled up and cried and cried.

I hid in this cave for some time. I began to imagine that I would never be able to leave this cave. My limping leg was so painful, that walking was impossible. In addition, the thought of falling or slipping or tumbling down a crevice darker and deeper than a bottomless hole paralyzed me with anxiety. I gave up hope.

I asked myself. "Why didn't my master fix my limp? He fixed Romey's sister's limp. Why not me? I will die all alone in this cave. My bones will never even be found for a proper burial." I lay down and gave myself up for dead.

I'm not sure how long

But on the coldest night I had

shaking so hard my teeth ch

There were ghostly creatures

The creatures were cold to t

around my shaking bones. They pulled ...,
screamed and wailed so loud that it could have wakened
the dead.

Then I thought, *Maybe I am dead. Are they waking
me?*

I begged for these spirits to leave me be. My
begging just made them worse. A group of them gathered
around, they poked me and demanded that I follow them.
They insisted I jump down a mountain crevice. They lured
me to follow them with songs and cooing noises.

They described my beautiful girlfriend, Romey,
and told me she would be at the bottom of the crevice to
welcome me. I was tempted. Before I rousted myself up, I
saw my master in a dream fashion.

I cried out to him: "Oh dear Master, I don't know
that I will be able to catch up to you. I am so weary I
cannot get up, but I want to let you know how much I love
you and how I did try so hard to find you. How I hoped
you would not be angry with me for disobeying your wish

Israel." I also asked him if I should follow was hearing.

en I asked him that question, a fierce wind blew the cave. It was so warm it felt like a summer sun. creatures haunting me spun and curled up like a aper on fire. The cave sizzled with sounds of their demise. When they were gone, my own bones felt warm and soothed. I moved, and for the first time in some weeks, the usual pain and agony had vanished.

I let my body rest for another day while I made my plans to set out first thing in the morning.

I woke up to the smell of camels. There is a certain essence from the leather and blankets hoisted atop their humped backs that is unmistakable. I also smelled spicy lentils and flat breads. There was even a hint of honey in the air. Honey dripping from clay pots. The tassel around my neck tickled my chin. My ears perked up. *Yes they are camel bells. So sweet.*

I stood up. I could stand without shaking and falling over. I sniffed the air again. *Yes eastward.* My nose told me to run eastward.

I was no longer afraid of falling. No longer did my paw feel lame. I felt like a gazelle or a cougar cat as I took off like a shooting star toward the east. I ran and ran down the mountain. It was as if a path had been cut out just for me. The moon went down and the sun arose and still I kept running.

When the mountains were behind me, a valley appeared. It was green and fertile. My paws were thankful for the soft earth and the cushions of sweet grass. It was sublime. The region stayed this way for several days. On the third day the land began to change and once again, I faced another desert before me. The winds were changing and spinning. The visibility became a great challenge. I had to stop and take cover. I hid behind a stonewall that had been wrecked and abandoned. It was crumbling and as the wind whipped through the region, the wall whistled and wailed. My eardrums hurt and my eyes were shut. My tassel and silk ribbon almost blew off of my neck. (I had lost so much weight that they were no longer fastened close to me.)

I stayed behind the wall until the winds calmed a bit. I pushed on despite the haze from all the whirlwinds. I was moving forward slowly, hardly able to see a foot in front of me, when I suddenly bumped into a warm-blooded creature.

"Ouch!"

It was a long legged camel. His head bent close to my head. He was so close I could smell his grassy breath. He nibbled at my ear. He said, "Watch it dog!"

I pardoned myself. "I am sorry. I have been traveling for a very long time in search of my master. I wonder if you know of him?"

The camel said, "Well who is your master and I will tell you."

"His name is Jesus."

The camel did something funny. He lowered his front legs and then lowered his back legs. We were practically eye-to-eye. "I know your master. He is way up at the head of the line. Hop on my back and I will take you to him."

I asked the camel, "Do I look all right? I want to look presentable."

He looked at me and told me I looked just fine.

I hopped on his back and we made our way past each camel and mule toward the front of the line. My heart was beating so fast. I had tears of anticipation running down my cheeks. I swallowed a million times on top of the gigantic camel's back.

Then...suddenly...my world lit up. I saw him.... My dear master.

My master saw this odd sight coming his way: a dog riding atop a camel's back. He squinted from the sun in his eyes.

Some of the nomads laughed.

I barked and wagged my tail. "Master. It is I. It is Issa. Your devoted dog."

He recognized me. He knew it was me. He smiled. "Issa. Issa. Is it you my dearest Issa?"

The camel bent his head low and made it manageable for me to jump down.

I ran straight into the arms of my friend my dearest master.

He held me tight. I licked him and licked him and when he let me down to get a good look at me, I jumped up and down and danced and rolled over.

He rubbed my ears and my chin. "How did you make this journey?"

I decided I would wait and tell him my stories for another day. For now we had miles and miles to go.... Together.

And this is how it came to pass that we visited the land of India. We walked through the great Himalayas. We traveled into Nepal and other lands of the Orient.

Our journey to many lands was filled with marvels, hardships, joy and strange, mystifying events. Yes, there are many stories yet to tell.

But on that day of our reunion, I walked proudly beside my master. And as the days and weeks, months and years went by, we watched over each other and had many happy nights under the great moons of the desert sky with the bells gently ringing, spicy lentils cooking and flat breads baking and the sweet smell of honey dripping from clay pots.

Yes, a joy to find him and rest sweet with him. And... a joy to one day return with him to our homeland.

I will tell my stories tomorrow, but for now I will rest. For now I will rest.

CHAPTER 2

We were in India just south of the Kashmir Pass. There was talk of Delhi some distance to the south, which we heard was big and raucous with many markets that sold food and wares to people from all over the known world.

We were just outside the city of Strinagar, the most beautiful city I have ever seen, except for, of course, our hometown of Nazareth. In Strinagar there are two lakes that are as blue as clear sapphire, and the white clouds that spec the turquoise sky look like fat sheep. There is a smell in the air of baking flat breads and homemade curries, and in the early afternoon, an intoxicating breeze full of sandalwood and rose fills the air.

As heavenly as this new land was, I could not enjoy it, not really. I was too busy worrying about my master's safety.

I refused to leave his side. I slept as close to him as I could. I followed him on his daily walks and sat beside him when he was studying or talking to his friends. His new friends were strange looking. They were Hindus and I was very wary of them.

Jesus encouraged me to relax and have fun with my new friends: Briden, the camel, and Mosey, the young donkey. But I didn't have time to play. Not that I wasn't tempted, especially when I could see Briden and Mosey having a good time by the stream or going off for a trot into the valley that surrounded our camp.

My new friends were different from any friends I had ever had before. Basically, Jesus and his family were my friends and, of course, my family in Jericho counted. Joseph and Mary had two cats that would, from time to time, pay attention to me, but other than my master and Romey, who I thought of everyday, I wasn't introduced to many other animals.

Briden was different because he was a camel. He was extremely tall, even by camel standards. He had exotic carpets and tassels that dangled from his leather saddle. His bridle was studded with turquoise and cherry red amber, and he enjoyed the privilege, from time to time, to carry my master. Mosey was a one-year-old donkey whose mother had died giving birth to her. The baby donkey survived and was given a boy's name by one of the nomads who hoped she was a boy. In some ways, I thought Mosey tried too hard to be a boy. She refused to wear colorful blankets or any ornamental flourish. She was the total opposite to Briden, who liked to dress up more that any other animal in the camp.

Briden had promised Mosey's mother, before she drew her last breath, that he would always protect and care for the orphan, and with that promise the mother closed her eyes in peace, knowing that Briden, a camel with a great intellect and upstanding character promised to be the caretaker of her baby girl.

Briden and I had a lot in common. He had Mosey and I had Jesus.

Mosey was always in mischief, and Briden was frequently in a state of anxiety over the little donkey. I would help when I could, and likewise, Briden would help me out with my master.

It was difficult to keep up with my master. Crowds of holy men started coming to our camp to hear him speak. I would sit proudly beside him during these times and sometimes the people would ask, "Is this your dog?"

Jesus would pat my head and rub my ears. "Yes, this is Issa."

Despite the crowds and people who seemed to follow us, he always found time for just the two of us. We would go on walks together everyday. During these walks he spoke aloud and asked me all kinds of baffling questions. I listened to his questions and was always glad he never pressed me to answer. It was almost as if someone else was there speaking back, but I never heard another voice or saw another soul. These conversations seemed to be followed by a period of rest. We would stop and lie down for a spell. He would sleep and I would watch over him.

On one of these occasions, when Jesus was resting, I heard a noise a small distance away. I trotted toward the sound, thinking it might be Mosey playing a trick on me. "Mosey, is that you Mosey?"

Suddenly, a stranger startled me from behind a stand of large rocks. He was wearing a heavy wool robe the color of wet sand and his fingers peaked through the long sleeves. His nose was long and his lips were black and he seemed to hiss when he moved.

The stranger laughed at me. He tried to catch me.

I brandished my teeth and snarled and ran in circles, making him bend and fall and look silly trying to catch me.

"Mind you dog, when I catch you, I'll skin your hide." He pulled a dagger out from his robe.

His voice was hoarse and filled with vicious words. He kept yelling at me. "Where is your master? Tell me and you won't get hurt."

He came toward me, his shiny blade aimed for my neck. He lunged for me and cuffed me by the scruff of my neck. I yelped and twisted my head practically backwards, trying to sink my teeth into his hand. I managed to break his skin, which felt dry and course. His blood smelled like the stench of old goat, and it didn't run red like most blood runs. It ran black and it curled and foamed like a stagnant brook.

He cursed me again and swung a hard blow to my head. I lost my balance and fell to the ground. It was then that I got a good look at his eyes, which were a green from the darkest place in the forest, almost black, and they dripped an ooze that stunk like his blood and stung my fur when it landed on my hind leg.

I mustered all the strength I could and hauled toward him. I felt his boney legs as I leapt upon him. Then, like a vapor, he disappeared. I fell to the ground. I looked about, but he was gone…vanished. All that was left of him was an unsavory smell. I heard a shake and looked fast enough to see a desert viper twist under some rocks and brush.

I took off toward my beloved master. He was awake by now and sitting on a large stone. Birds were singing around him, as was often the case. I feared for his life, knowing that he could easily be caught unawares.

"Arff."

There it was, the slithering thing: Shiny and green, sparkling in the rays of sunlight, the viper was getting closer and closer to my master. I flew through the air and snarled at the cold-blooded thing.

I tore my teeth into the viper's body. A taste like rotten fruit spewed into my mouth. My tongue seemed to catch fire, but I held on. The viper and I wrestled and spun in the air and onto the ground. I would not let go. He eventually fell limp in my mouth.

When my master carried me back to camp I was cold and stiff.

Briden cried every time he told the story: "Your master brought you back to where Mosey and I were resting. He placed you on a swatch of woven cloth and pulled your ears back. He was kneeling close to you and spoke into your ears. Then he laid his hands over your heart." Briden would swallow hard and go on, "Mosey was trying to be brave and not cry, and I was sobbing, to think you were gone. Then, of course, when I noticed the viper's bite on your neck, my heart despaired. Your master, dear Issa, was bent over you as he put his hands on your bite. Suddenly, your stiffness turned soft and your coldness turned warm. Your eyes opened and your let out the sweetest whimper any animal has whimpered before or since."

I was glad that Briden recalled that awful night with such detail, for I could not remember much about it. When I came back to the world of the living, what I do remember was my master putting his own blanket over me, and that he slept beside me the whole night.

Several days later, I told Briden about the strange man who turned into a snake. I was feeling much better and wondered if Briden would believe me or not. His nostrils flared when I told him about the horrible stink.

And what he told me next, after he stopped shaking long enough himself, was that no matter how dead I thought the snake was…he wasn't. This was the last thing I wanted to hear.

He explained to me as calmly as he knew how. "Issa, they are not of this world. They are dark spirit. The viper you tore apart was the devil himself."

He stomped the sand and his head whisked from side to side. He moved in a circle and then dipped and bent into his kneeling position. We were at eye level.

He went on, "You can always tell by the stench. It's a decrepit and sulfuric rot straight from the underworld itself."

I was frightened more than ever. I had heard the word devil, but only thought it a passing fancy for storytellers.

"Oh Issa, the devil is very real." Then Briden added, "He stinks to high heaven." He repeated that again, "He stinks to high heaven."

Briden told me that the devil was out to get us because my master was so good and kind.

I was shaking by this time so Briden put one of his small woolen carpets on my back. He smiled his sweet camel smile. "Don't despair Issa. You will always be at an

31

advantage because of your keen nose and now you know exactly how your enemy smells. And the devil can be smelled a mile away. You and your master are safe…for now."

I took comfort in his words and decided I was at an advantage, at least for now.

What took possession of my dreams for some weeks was the notion that this thing could not be killed. That is what kept me up at night.

Some weeks went by, and as time passed, I began to relax and forget about the imminent danger of my stinky enemies. Larger crowds were coming to listen to my master. They camped along the hillsides close to our camp. They traveled from all over India to see him, for word had spread about this very young man who knew so much. The crowds marveled at him: "He is just a boy really. Where did he learn? He knows things about the mysteries of life that even the elders cannot know."

I never thought about my master being young or old. I know when I watched him sleep that his face was always peaceful. He did not yet have a beard like the grown men did, but he seemed older in spirit than most.

Very often at night when he would sit and listen to the nomads sing, a white band of light would appear over his head. This arch of light made anyone close by feel safe and warm, and in the cold shade of the moon it seemed very much like heaven. With all the studying and speaking that his daily life demanded, his capacity to spend time with me became less and less.

During this period of days Briden would tell me stories. One day he asked me if I knew what an elephant was.

I told him, "I have never heard of such a thing."

Briden went on, "They are the biggest animals around. They're not as tall as the giraffes I have seen, but in shear weight, no animal can match them. They have a nose as long as the sleeve of a giant, and they can blow water from it as if from a waterfall."

I didn't believe him.

He told Mosey and me this story: "I once met a Hindu elephant that had a small tent set up on his back. Two children and their mother lived in this tent and when it came time for them to bathe, the elephant would lumber to the clear creek near our camp and spray them with fresh water. The children would stand on his backside just behind the small tent and laugh so hard they would practically fall off. I watched this go on day after day, and finally I came up to the elephant and asked him if would mind giving me a bath. He asked me to follow him, which I did and when we came to the banks of the creek. He filled his long grey trunk with the water. Oh dear children, it was wonderful, the spray from his trunk, cascading over my tired back. I should like to see another elephant again before I am dead and gone."

Mosey and I loved the story, as he told it quite often. Briden loved elephants and wanted us to be able to see one. We loved the story until he came to the end and said the part about wanting to see one before he was dead and gone. This always made Mosey sad. She would try and cover her ears, which was next to impossible.

Despite the story of the kind Hindu elephant, I was still suspicious of the lot.

Briden would say, "Your master Jesus isn't afraid of the Hindus. Don't you think that your master, with all his wisdom, would know if these people meant him harm?"

Briden's logic was sound, but the memories of the thieves that captured me and almost boiled me for a stew was still fresh on my mind.

Briden would scream, "But the thieves that captured you were not Hindus! And besides Hindus don't eat meat!"

I hoped he was right.

One day, I decided to be brave. I asked the Hindu cook who worked for the Brahmins; "May I take a peek in your stew pot?"

The Hindu, who wore a white gauze turban on his head, replied, "Why of course you can look into my stew pot."

I peered into the pot. I asked, "What? No meat? "

The Hindu cook laughed at me and said, "No. No. Rice and saffron, carrots, onions and beautiful orange lentils." He reached into a cloth bag full of lentils, sifting them through his hands as if it were gold.

When I told the story later that day to Briden, he said that the only one who should fear a Hindu is a vegetable.

For a number of days I sniffed around the stand of rocks where my life almost came to end. I sniffed everywhere until my neck began to ache and the tip of my nose began to bleed. I felt sickly after my empty search, so I kept quiet and still for a few days.

One starry night, when I knew my master was safely asleep in his tent, Briden and Mosey and I huddled very close together on a patch of old carpets that the nomad people had laid out for us. A cold eastern breeze had blown in from the desert and the wind whistled around and through the camp. Briden waited for Mosey to start snoring, and when he was absolutely sure that Mosey was deep in sleep, he began to tell me a story. Briden made sure his voice was low, almost a whisper. "Issa, this is meant just for your ears."

I moved in closer to hear him.

He paused to cover Mosey with a blanket. "I have seen something in the stars."

Briden was a very smart camel. He listened well to many of the sages and scholars he had met on the trails and over time came to understand how to read the night sky and interpret what some of the Indian holy men were saying about my master.

I asked him to explain: "What Briden? What have you learned? "

Briden looked at the young Mosey with great affection. He cleared his throat before he went on in a whisper. "Mosey, it's about Mosey." He paused again. "Our dear Mosey will play a very important role in your master's future."

"Like what? What do you mean?" I inquired.

Briden replied, "When Mosey is grown up, she will carry your master on her back and crowds of people will throw Palm leaves on the path before them. They will enter a great city together."

I was not particularly beside myself with joy about this vision Briden had had. I blurted it out, "Will I be there? "

Briden pushed me with his big head and smiled his peculiar smile that spread from one ear to another, "Yes, Issa. I see you there. You will be at her side."

Then I asked Briden, "What about you Briden? Will you be there? You will be there, won't you?

Briden kept a smile on his face but didn't answer me for a moment. He just said, "I can't say for sure. But it's too soon to worry about that for now. Let's get some sleep and dream of coconut milk and desert flowers."

And that's what I did. I dreamed of warm desert nights and luscious coconut milk straight from it's cracked brown shell.

*****

Briden was a very helpful friend when it came to my anxiety; however, he had anxieties of his own. Due to his promise to keep Mosey safe and raise her as his own, he worried most of the time. Even after his vision, he remained ever steady in his care of her, but Mosey was precocious. At times she would purposefully hide from Briden and me to create a stir.

I thought Briden was overly protective and told him so. "Maybe you should let Mosey wander a bit more without such concern. Everyone in the camp knows her and will make sure no harm comes her way. Maybe if you weren't so worried she wouldn't be so naughty. "

"Oh, you're a fine one to talk. Maybe you should practice what you preach. "

I liked the sound of practicing what I preached and that is when I began to wander on my own. Briden's prophecies of the future made me more confident and less worrisome about my master. I decided to have a little fun for myself.

*****

The very next day I trotted into the city of Srinagar all by myself. Without much effort I came across a very strange site. There was a man lying on the side of the road with a crowd gathered around him. This man was lying on a bed of very spiked thorns, which seemed to be as comfortable as a feather bed to him.

I asked myself. "How could this man be so comfortable?"

Before I had time to think, he answered me. He lifted his head from the queer mattress and said. "It's really easy."

I jumped back with a start. *Someone who spoke the dog language besides my master?*

I told the man that he should be ashamed of himself, having people believe he was so powerful and brave that even sharp thorns were pleasurable. I suspected the thorns were padded with a soft tip and his tomfoolery, to me, was inexcusable.

"If you don't believe, why don't you lay down on it for yourself?" he quipped.

This man, who I later learned was a Sadhu, got up from his bed of thorns and beseeched me to lie on the brambles. The crowd stared at me. What could I do? I had challenged the Sadhu for being a fake. The crowd began to taunt me.

"Go ahead see for yourself," he urged.

My honor was at stake. I decided that I would teach this man a lesson. I set my gaze on the nest of brambles and thorns, confident that there was trickery involved. I walked bravely toward the spiked mattress.

The moment I touched the mat I regretted my arrogance. I yelped a yelp that rang throughout the crowd.

A woman next to me pushed me deeper upon the bed.

The sharp thorns pricked into my paws. I lost balance and my body heaved to the left. That is when the thorns tore into the skin on my belly and dug into my sides under my fur. I cried out of help.

The Sadhu put his hand on my head. I became as still as a statue. I could not budge. He lifted me into his arms. He carried me to a nearby well and pulled water up from a bucket attached to a rope. He cradled me and washed my paws in the cool water.

I felt ashamed for the arrogance and judgment I had weighed against him.

He petted me and said, "I forgive you." Then he laughed. He continued,

"The power of the mind is a mystery. When you learn to use it, even your enemies will bow before you."

I thought about the stinky viper and the man with the dagger. I asked him.

"What is your name?"

" My name is Sundar," he answered. There was a twinkle in his eye.

I invited him back to the camp. I wanted him to meet my master. He agreed and we began our walk back to the hillsides outside of town. He was a most interesting looking man. He wore a yellow robe made of cotton and his forehead was painted with three white stripes that ran from temple to temple. His hair was matted and piled high on top of his head. He was thin and his fingernails were long and somewhat curved. He had a long beard that met his chest and his voice was rather high-pitched.

We finally reached camp. I spotted Mosey and Briden near a small pond some distance away from the tents. They saw me as I approached with my new friend Sundar.

Briden had been worried and spoke out before I had time to introduce the Sadhu. "Issa, where have you been? I have been so worried. "

Mosey had been worried as well, I could tell by the look on her face. Her ears were stretched back and she brayed loudly.

I looked up at Sundar. "This is my new friend."

Briden and Mosey were impressed with the Sadhu's dramatic appearance.

"Let's take my new friend to meet my master," I insisted.

Mosey and Briden took the lead towards the front of the camp. Sundar and I followed close behind.

We stopped for a sip of water and some rice at the campfire. After we ate, Briden kneeled low and let Sundar ride on his back. My master was some distance away in a valley between two hills. We traveled for about half an hour.

I finally saw him. I was so excited I jumped up on Mosey and did some tricks and twirls on her back. When Jesus spotted me he started laughing and let me jump into his arms.

He could tell I was in great anticipation and asked me," What is it Issa? What cannot wait?"

I let him know there was someone I wanted him to meet. He looked around and saw Mosey and Briden, but there was no Sundar.

My master had been speaking to a crowd of the Hindu holy men. They were dressed in white and had been intently listening to my master until I burst in. They ignored me and begged my master to continue with his discourse.

Jesus looked at the crowd and explained that he could not continue until he had helped me find my lost friend. And at that, we all set off to find Sundar.

Briden explained to us, "He jumped down from my back, and that's a mighty leap. He didn't even wait for me to kneel. He took off and vanished into the forest."

We walked slowly through the woods. Briden had to duck so as not to get too scratched up from the low thick branches. I led the way with Jesus at my tail. Mosey was behind Jesus and Briden held the rear. We walked quietly for some time. The owls and other screeching birds swooped and looped around us. Small eyes from behind trees and low bushes watched as we went deeper and deeper into the forest.

A small dear ran across our path. He looked at us and said, "Follow me."
We followed him and a beautiful light emerged to lead our way. Soon we were in a green valley where giant lilies and enormous leaves engulfed us. The air became fragrant with the scents of blooming wildflowers and strange plants. The deer had stayed close to my master so they were, by now, leading the way. The deer led to a cave. There was singing coming from inside.

We entered the cave so quietly that even the spiders and bats ignored us. We simply followed the singing, and before long, all of us stopped in our tracks.

There was Sundar floating some distance off the floor of the cave. His legs were crossed and his hands were set in a strange fashion.

He continued chanting his lovely song. He floated in the air and then slowly, as he noticed us gawking at him, lowered himself down to the floor of the cave. I was so happy to see Sundar that I didn't even bother to ask him he how he was able to float in midair. Instead I blurted out, "What happened Sundar, why did you leave?"

Sundar turned to my master and spoke, "When I saw the group of Brahmins around you, I became afraid and ran away. These men that come to hear you are another kind of holy men. These men study and are considered the great intellectuals of my country. They are a high caste of men and are to be honored and revered. And to see that they are coming to you to learn and to ask you about your ideas made me afraid, so I ran."

I had to ask him before any one had a chance to respond, "But what about you? "

Sundar held my paw and explained, "I was from the Brahmin caste, but I chose the life of a Sadhu. I survive only by the alms that come my way. I am matted and unrinsed. Some are afraid of me. They think I mingle in dark magic and make curses and fool nature with my eyes."

At that moment I remembered Sundar floating in mid air and asked him,

"Were you really floating or was that a trick?"

Sundar answered, " No, No. That was not a trick. That is a power—a power of mind over body."

I looked at master and asked him if he could float in mid-air?

He simply answered me, "If it was necessary."

I immediately wanted to learn how to lift myself from the ground but was warned by Sundar that personal power must be a carefully learned process.

Jesus rubbed my head and assured me that maybe one day I would know how to perform such extraordinary feats.

Briden and Mosey were struck silent.

Sundar hung his head and spoke again, "I am sorry I caused such a stir. I did not want to shame you or create problems, but these men that seek you out are the finest thinkers in our land."

I spoke up and told him that my master had taught me not to judge and to love all men equally. I assured him that the Brahmins were no better or worse than any of us.

My words hung in the damp cave. There was a silence and all eyes were on me: Briden, Mosey, my master, and even Sundar. It was as if all the eyes in the caves, from the spiders, the bats and all the creepy crawly things that lived there were staring at me.

I even started looking at myself. There, I said it: All men are equal and all men are to be loved the same. This made all my fears and all my squawking about the strangers seem small and not right. I felt a happiness inside me.

Master petted my head and Briden gave me a kindly nudge with his nose.

Master then came forward and kneeled close to Sundar, "Don't be afraid or ashamed."

Sundar asked my master, "Who are you that the wise men from my country come to you? Where are you from? "

My master answered him, "My name is Jesus and I come from Nazareth."

At this Sundar threw himself at my master's feet. He began to weep.

My master became quiet and then asked Sundar, "Why do you weep? "

Sundar looked up. The three stripes of white paint across his forehead sparkled. "I am Sundar, the son of Melchoir the Magi."

We all stood quietly as Sundar continued, "It was my father Melchoir who left our county some years ago in search of a king in a faraway land. My father and two other Magi followed a star. They left in the summer of one year and faithfully followed the heavenly light. They met all kinds of danger and mysteries on their journey, but never gave up. Many months later, they found the king. He was an infant, in a humble place, nothing that even remotely resembled a royal birth; yet still, my father and the other magi knew they were in the right place. They had carried frankincense, myrrh and other precious gifts to this holy child. My father and the other two met the parents of this child. They were allowed to see the baby and they bowed before him."

My master moved in closer to Sundar, as Sundar looked into my master's eyes and said, "The child's name was Jesus." Sundar lowered his eyes and kissed my master's hand.

Briden, Mosey and I listened intently to the Sadhu's story.

Then my master asked, "Is your father still alive? "

"Yes, he is still alive, although he is very old. He lives in Nepal, high in the Himalayas."

Jesus spoke, "I would like to go to this place and meet your father."

Sundar smiled. " It would be a great honor to take you."

We left the dark forest and made our way back to camp. The Brahmins were still settled in the hills around our camp. When they saw us approaching with Sundar, they stood up and asked my master what he was doing cavorting with a yellow robed Sadhu.

One Brahmin stood up and said, "Some of the Sadhu's are trouble to our community. They can bring on curses and cause many problems."

Sundar looked down for he was once again shameful.

My master faced the crowd and spoke, "This Sadhu is a good man. He has chosen a lonely and difficult life. Judging others is a waste of precious time."

All became silent and the lofty Brahmins became ashamed of their arrogance.

Again, my master addressed the crowd, "We are traveling soon to Nepal. Which ones among you will accompany us on our journey?"

One man in the crowd cried out, "You are going to travel to Nepal with a Sadhu, a donkey, a camel and a dog?"

They had not yet learned the message from my master. Other men were yelling, "You are mad! Surely you will all die. This is no journey for a circus!"

My master spoke softly, "We will find the Magi that found me so many years ago. This journey is blessed."

At that, several of the men familiar with the mountainous route volunteered to assist us.

CHAPTER 2

And so our journey into the Himalayas began.

CHAPTER 3

The first few days of our trip were perfect, as if a heavenly magistrate had designed the weather and traveling conditions for us. Mosey and I teamed up with the first leg of the pack, and Briden, due to his size, was well behind us.

I knew that Briden was fearful about the trip. He told me on the night before we were to depart, "Issa, I feel that the journey might not be good for me."

I asked him, "What do you mean? You have traveled back and forth again many times over the desert. You have seen marvels from all corners of the earth. Why Briden, why the second-guessing?"

He hung his head and his body trembled before he answered my question. He said, "Once upon a time, many years ago, I heard stories about a creature that lived in the Himalayas that drank camels' blood for breakfast. And if the rains did not come in the summer months, the creature ripped off their humps with his bare hands and stored them away in the back of his cave for water."

I was suddenly seized with my own terror and asked him, "What does he do with dogs? "

Briden popped back, " Nothing, he does nothing with dogs—nothing with donkeys—nothing with men. He only eats camels. That's my point!"

49

"But Briden, why would anyone eat camels?"

Briden got square with my eyes and made me promise not to tell a soul.

I assured him: "I promise. I promise never to tell a soul."

Then he whispered, "Camel's blood is good luck."

"Good luck?"

"Shhhhhh."

Briden admonished me and hushed me again: "Shhhhhh." He looked around and practically sat on me before he said, "No one must know."

I thought I would trick Briden into not being afraid. So I said to him, "Briden, what if the summer has brought much rainfall? "

He knew the answer. " Not so," he said, "I have heard some of the animals coming back from the mountains saying that, so far, the season is very dry. Good for traveling, but not good for the creature's blood lust. I heard a story yesterday that two camels went missing from a trade caravan through the Himalayas. They disappeared into thin air." He paused and went on, "I can tell you where they went. They went straight into the creatures cave. He is probably drinking their blood at this very moment."

I spoke up, "Then I am going to tell master and Sundar about this creature so they can rid the mountains of such an evil beast."

Briden all but sat on top of me again. "No. No. You must not tell anyone, not your master or Sundar or any human. They do not believe animal stories. They would just think I was possessed or mad."

Briden had a point. The story was hard to swallow, even for me. I promised Briden to keep my mouth shut about the creature, but I also assured him that I would be vigilant in my search for any signs of the camel eater as we made our way through the mountains.

I asked him, "Has anyone ever seen the creature? Do we know what he looks like or smells like?"

Briden said, "He looks like a giant man covered in red fur, and he has no smell." Then he paused… and spoke again, "At least your enemy has a smell. This creature is very clever. He smells like the air of the rhododendron forests and the fragrant grass of the mountain valleys. He rubs his back with the leaves and rolls in the meadows so no one can detect his coming."

I was saddened by Briden's dilemma. I suggested that he stay behind in Srinigar and that on our return homeward we would reunite with him.

He answered, "No, I must go. I hear that elephants live in Pokhara, just outside of Katmandu, and I have been waiting to see them for a long time."

So at that, we set out on our journey the next morning; I, with my secret about the creature that ate camels, and Briden with his terror of meeting up with the beast. We decided to hold a stoic posture so that no one could detect what we both held deep inside.

Mosey was oblivious to our anxiety. She played and showed her daring every chance she could. We were a group of about twenty and on the third day of travel, we split into two separate groups so the big animals could take an easier path.

The Sherpa in charge, an older man named Ram, insisted I be a part of the shortcut group along with my master. I was worried for Briden as they separated us. I watched the second group travel northeast, I looked at Briden and he at me, and we both wished each other good stead. My heart was heavy, for I wondered if the camel eater would snag him… and my best friend would be gone forever.

Later that day, as we traveled through a rather craggy trail, I imagined that my good friend was safe and well looked after. It was the only way to adjust my mood, because anxiety is a deadly emotion to have on a mountain slope. Travel in the mountains requires steadfast mindfulness and acute attention to the next step.

Everything was going rather well until I saw the thing in front of me. Nothing like I had ever seen before.

The suspension bridge strapped from one peak to another. The length of it, the shaky expanse of it, was more daunting than anything I had ever seen. The bridge was swinging and swaying from the Himalayan wind, which liked to take the fur right off my hide.

My master followed three Sherpas across the bridge. When my turn came to step onto the bamboo bridge, I stopped dead in my tracks and headed back for the edge of the bluff. The floor of the bridge was slick from the spray of the rapids below, and so narrow that one foot had to go in front of the other, as if walking on a tight rope.

No one ahead of me noticed that I had not started out across the bridge.

The sound of the rushing river below was so loud that even if I barked my very loudest, I would not have been heard. The wind was howling and blowing so fierce that the gusts liked to lift me straight into the air. The spray from the rapids was freezing cold, and my fur was soaking wet.

After what seemed like an endless string of moments, I saw my master and the group of Sherpas reach the other side. I recognized my master because he had a rose colored sash thrown over his shoulder. One of the Sherpa's wives had given it to him before we set out on the journey. I saw his figure turn around, expecting me to be right there, but I was not.

My master and I locked eyes with a quarter of a mile of shaky bamboo between us. The weather was beginning to change and the afternoon storms that frequented the mountains of the Himalayas were upon us. The sky went gray. The wind churned and howled. The bridge flipped over from the gusts. I wanted to cry.

I saw the three Sherpas jumping up and down and holding their fur hats tight to their heads. They appeared to be arguing. My master was untwisting the bridge and one of the Sherpas was holding on to him so he would not blow over the side of the mountain.

I would have wailed if I could have been heard. I would have begged my master not to return across the bridge, but, as sure as moss on a river stone, he was heading back for me.

The late afternoon storm was fierce and the visibility was next to nothing. I could make out the rose-colored sash, blowing and twirling upwards towards the low clouds, which began to blanket us. After some time, I could make out his figure. His voice rose above the roar. He said, "Issa, don't be afraid."

I felt ashamed. What if my Jesus had slipped and plunged into the raging rapids toward sure death? I would never have been able to live it down.

I said to him, "Master, I am sorry. My courage abandoned me. I failed you."

He wasn't angry one bit. He simply lifted me up from off the edge of the bluff and strapped me to his back with the rose sash. Step by slippery step he carried me across to the other side.

When we reached the other side, one of the Sherpas untied me from the rose sash and set me on the ground. My master kneeled in front of me and dried me off with the hem of his soft wool robe. He said, "You're safe now Issa."

I thanked him, reminding him that once again I was forever in his debt.

The Sherpas weren't so kind. They scolded me: "You could have been the cause of your kind master's death. We are going to leave you at the next village so you will not ruin our journey!"

The oldest one, Ram, spoke up, "We cannot have a cowardly dog on our trek. This is dangerous business, and if you hinder one man, you hinder us all!"

I crawled under my master's robe. I wished the earth would take one big swallow of me and that would be the end of it. But the earth did not take its bite of me.

CHAPTER 3

Instead I heard my master say to them, "Please forgive my
Issa. He is still a young dog and perhaps we should have
kept better watch over him."

The youngest Sherpa, Orif, lifted me up on his
shoulders and pranced me around. My master could not
help but smile and shake his head. I stayed on top of Orif's
shoulders and thanked the Himalayan stars that I was safe.
That night when we set up our camp, I snuck under my
master's covers and swore to him, once again, that I would
protect him to the very end of my days, forever and ever.
And at that, I fell sound asleep under the cold Himalayan
heavens.

The next morning the air was filled with icy
crystals, even though the sun was shining. My fur was
warm, but the ice crystals blowing about were so cold they
stung my nose and ears. The crystals became like
thousands of prisms floating about, so for some time I
chased the dancing specks of purple, yellow, orange and
pale green. The camp was busy, making ready for our
day's journey while I chased the tiny rainbows.

I was excited that morning, most of all because we
were to meet up with the others. My anticipation about
seeing Briden was great. I could not wait to see him with
his colorful blankets and stacks of heavy cargo that had
been strapped to his wonderful humped back. My secret
about the camel-eating creature was almost more than I

could bear. On two different occasions I was tempted to tell my master, but my good sense prevailed and I managed to keep silent. I comforted myself with the thought that Briden did have Sundar in his group and that Sundar was keen to the ways of the Himalayas and the creatures that might lurk. Maybe even Sundar knew of this camel-eating beast and would look for any signs that it might be close by.

Finally, my group set out after a good breakfast of dried fish and goat cheese. It was a perfect day for traveling through the mountain passes.

We stopped for a short rest at noon and as if from nowhere as many as twenty men, dressed in bright orange and yellow robes, chanting in a deep and resonant sound, approached us.

They were a happy lot and stopped to share some rice with us. After we ate with these men, they invited us to follow them to their dwelling place. The Sherpas kept bowing to the men and my master accepted their invitation.

When I found out about our change of plans, I ran to my master. I barked as loud as I could to get his attention.

He looked at me and asked, "What is it Issa? What is all the commotion about?"

I told him that a detour would be rude. "Briden, Mosey and Sundar are going to be disappointed if we are delayed."

By this time the orange and yellow robed men, who I later found out were monks, asked my master, "What is wrong with the dog? He seems most upset."

My master looked at them and explained, "Issa, my dog, is afraid it might be rude to delay our meeting. His best friends are with the others and he has missed them."

The monks looked at me, and several of them got on their knees next to me. They spoke to the Sherpas in their language and before long the whole group of them were pointing to a mountain close by.

I heard Orif translating to my master what the monks had said to the older Sherpas. "The monks are Buddhists and they felt great compassion with Issa's concern about the others in the group. They know a short cut through the valley near their monastery that will lead to our meeting place."

So that was how it happened that we went to the great monastery in the mountains. When we arrived at the monastery a chorus of monks sang. Their singing echoed throughout the valley and if they weren't singing they were playing on bells, blowing through giant horns, or thumping on very low-tuned drums. This music was like no music I had ever heard before.

I had never seen a place so big. The monastery had open hallways and stairways that the mountain winds whistled through. There were big rooms and small rooms; there were chambers below other chambers, and from almost all points, the tall peaks of the Himalayas could be seen. The wind and low-riding clouds blew and drifted through the rooms and open courtyards as if they were playing a game of chase.

My master was taken to the leader of the monks. I had been asked to wait by a staircase until one of the younger monks arrived. I waited and waited and started to get very sleepy. I fell asleep.

*****

When I woke up, I felt very much alone. I began looking for my master. I was anxious to get started again for our reunion with Briden, Mosey and Sundar.

I went down the staircase where I had been waiting. I found baskets of stored rice and wooden bowls full of root vegetables that looked freshly harvested. They smelled like earth and I could not resist the urge to take a bite. It was bitter so I spit it out. The taste of anything, no matter how bitter, reminded me how hungry I was.

I wandered into another chamber that was a few steps down from the storage room. A long dark hallway came off the second chamber and I slowly walked its length. I peeked into some small carved out passages and found one to be most interesting. There were some arched windows where sunshine and a nice breeze flowed through. I noticed some wooden boxes carved in various shapes on the floor of the room. I began to sniff them and managed to gently lift the lid off one of the boxes that was elaborately painted. The lid of the box hit the floor and made a sound that startled me. Although the room was quite dark, I began to make out the contents of the box.

Inside this box, arranged neatly, were five or six bones. I remembered my hunger and I had a distant memory of Joseph giving me some bones back in Nazareth. I sat at first and just looked at them. I wondered what on earth the monks did with the bones. *Maybe they used them for a savory broth?* I stretched my neck close and tasted the largest bone. I didn't have to think too much about it before I took the best looking one in my mouth and made way for daylight. After several wrong turns I finally found my way out to the courtyard. I trotted until I found a nice tree. That is where I gnawed on my trophy. When I was satisfied, I took care to bury my bone under the tree for safekeeping. At that, I set out to find Jesus.

I used my nose to find master. He was with a large group of monks and they were pouring over a stack of old books. The monks were showing my master page after page of elaborate drawings and beautifully written verses.

No one noticed when I entered the room. I wagged my tail and sniffed the hems of many robes, but my presence was of little concern to anyone. My master petted my head briefly, almost absent-mindedly. There were low murmurs amongst them and an occasional giggle. I sat off to the side hoping that my presence would eventually be noticed and it would dawn on my master and Ram that it was time to go.

One of the oldest monks took the lead towards the open archway and a small group of younger monks, my master, and Ram followed. I took off behind them. They went down the staircase where I had waited and had fallen asleep earlier. They continued down the very same path way that I had taken. Then we were in the room with the wonderfully painted boxes.

The oldest monk looked at the box that I had discovered earlier. There was a collective gasp in the room. The lid I had managed to lift off was still on the floor and the one bone I had taken became the object of much concern and unhappiness.

My master asked the monk, "What is wrong? Why are you so distraught?"

The monk explained, "This room is where we keep our relics. And the bone of one of our dearest monks has been taken. These relics have power and we use them in our most sacred ceremonies. The bone that is gone has been here for over four hundred and fifty years. This monk actually walked with the Buddha."

I let out a small whimper that again no one noticed. I started to pant.

My master looked at me and I looked at him and he knew. He knelt down to my level and asked me in a whisper, "Issa do you know anything about the missing bone?"

I wanted to tell him no. I wanted to run away at top speed. Instead, I looked into his eyes and then I lowered my head. I could not lie to him.

When he understood completely that I had taken the bone, he called the group of monks to order. They were looking around the chamber and wondering what spirit had swept off with the sacred bone.

Jesus said, "Dear monks. Dear monks. I am afraid I know where the bone is."

Ram translated to the monks what Jesus said.

They collectively stopped looking for the bone and stared silently at my master. When he had their full attention, he simply looked at them and said, "My dog Issa has taken the bone."

Ram yelled at me, "How could you do this? How could you steal holy relics? Are you a mad dog?"

My master calmed the group down as best he could. He asked me, "Issa, can you show us where you put the bone or did you eat it all?"

I sat up and barked.

My master said, "He wants us to follow him."

I darted out of the chamber with eleven monks, Ram and my master following close behind.

I ran through the hallways and anti chambers. I ran through the courtyard and out to the forest with the monks in able pursuit.

I found the tree that had underneath its roots the most sacred bone in all of Buddhism. I dug it up while the group looked on. I found it just as I left it, not as white, and not short of teeth marks.

I presented it to the head monk.

He took the sacred bone from my mouth. He inspected it carefully. And then he did a very strange thing. He started laughing. He laughed and he laughed. And when he laughed all the other monks laughed. And then my master smiled and started laughing. The only one who did not laugh was Ram, who had it out for me even worse that ever.

The monk took the bone back to its resting place. He said, "We are just happy to have our bone back, even if it does have the marks of Issa's teeth upon it."

Of course he spoke in his native language, but everyone seemed to understand. He told me that my life would be a happy one because I had taken a bite of the venerable monk that walked with the Buddha. I never knew who this Buddha was, but I was thankful that they were such a forgiving lot.

"Issa is dog nature, and a dog's nature is to find bones and bury them."

I heard this as Ram translated it to my master. He did so in a manner very stripped of ease. Ram, the old Sherpa, was embarrassed by my behavior. My master told me later that he was glad I had not lied to him about the bone, but that the greater lesson was to never take anything that was not mine, no matter how great the temptation.

I lay down at the entrance of the courtyard fully expecting a nudge when the time to go had come. I could not stop thinking about the bone and what the monk had said about my dog nature. I was different from humans. It was my nature to eat bones and it was their nature to worship them. The more I thought about my nature, the sleepier I became.

Just as I was about to nod off, a blast of horns commenced. The sound startled me. I jumped up to see what all the commotion was about. I ran to the open gate and saw what can only be described as a sight for sore eyes. There in the distance was a group of monks leading Briden, Mosey, Sundar and some other Sherpas toward the monastery. Orif was sitting on top of Briden and was waving at me.

There were three monks on top of the monastery's stone tower blowing away through very large curved horns.

I took off toward my friends. Briden and Mosey were trotting fast towards me, and Orif was bouncing so high that he almost fell off. When I reached them my heart was beating fast and my joy could not be contained.

Not long after that my master joined us. He said to me, "Issa, the young monks that took compassion on the concern you showed toward your friends decided to surprise you."

That evening we stayed at the monastery to eat and rest. We enjoyed the monks, and the monks enjoyed us. We promised to visit them again and when morning broke the next day, we set off for Pokhara.

*****

It was the best morning of the Himalayan trek because Briden let me ride on his back, and Sundar walked beside Mosey. My master was very happy that we were all together again, and for now I knew that Briden was safe from the beast.

It took many days to reach the city of Pokhara, which was surrounded by forests of Rhododendron and lakes so clear the fishes could be seen from the shores.

As we entered the city, crowds of people started gathering to greet us. An elder from the town led us to an impressive structure where Melchoir was waiting.

When Sundar saw his father, he couldn't contain his excitement and ran to embrace him. Melchoir was a very old man and had a white beard that fell to his waist. Their reunion was very touching and I couldn't help but wonder if my master would soon miss his own father Joseph.

Melchoir turned to my master and bowed. He said, "I have a surprise for you."

He clapped his hands together and from behind a curtain made from silk, two very old men emerged. They were dressed in royal garments and approached my master with the utmost curiosity.

As they reached my master, they bowed. The younger of the two said, "I am Caspar and when I first saw you as an infant I knew you were very special. I brought your family frankincense signifying your divine nature."

Then the second man approached. He was older than Caspar and younger than Melchoir. He had black hair and a black beard. He said, "I am Balthasar and I brought your family myrrh, signifying that you are also mortal and born among men."

The two men stepped back and then Melchoir spoke, "I am Melchoir, and I brought your family gold, signifying that you are a king."

I had never thought of my master as being a king before. He never dressed in silks and finery, and he never wore a crown on his head. He was poor and I thought that these wise men had my master mixed up with another somebody. I couldn't contain myself so I started barking.

Sundar, like my master, understood my state of bewilderment. He said, "Father, explain to Issa what it means to be a king."

Melchoir looked at me. He had a twinkle in his eye as he spoke, "Dear little Issa dog, being King of a country is different from being a King of men. I was born of royal lineage, but your master was born of the divine matter that comes straight from heaven. And the crown that he wears is pure light that not all people are able to see."

I looked at my master, and yes, it was true that very often a halo of light surrounded his head. I had noticed it before, and at that moment his halo of light was very bright. This explanation made me happy enough. I nudged the hem of my master's robe and he stroked my head sweetly.

My master thanked the three men and explained to them how much their gifts meant to his parents. He said to them, "My mother, Mary, will be very happy that I had this opportunity to meet you and thank you for your generosity and kindness."

Melchoir said, "We shall celebrate together for now." We entered a large room with a table full of fruits, cheeses and curried rice. After we ate, Melchoir led us out to the great courtyard where the stars could be seen, clear as a bell. There were elaborate rugs on the stone floor of the courtyard. We laid down to take in the fullness of the sky.

Melchoir looked at the sky and spoke to my master, "The star that led us to you can still be seen." He pointed to a corner of the sky that lit up like the morning sun as if his finger had commanded it.

I overheard Melchoir say to my master, "Dearest Jesus, according to the stars, it is time to return to your homeland. The light of the star that led us to you will lead you safely back home."

Ram told my master that it would take a week to gather supplies and make ready for the journey. The Sherpas would stay with us through the mountains and then we would hook up with a caravan near the Kashmir Pass.

During the week of preparation, my master spent most of his time with the three kings. I decided to explore the region with Briden and Mosey. Orif made sure he was with us the day we set out to see the great waterfall.

We were about an hour outside of the city when the roar from the falls could be heard.

There was a mist as we approached the falls. The valley we were in was covered with wild flowers and the air almost stung with perfume. My vision was hindered from the spray of the falls. I turned around to see Briden with his eyes squint, struggling to see the ground in front of him. As I watched him struggle, I suddenly saw his struggle turn into a delighted rapture. I turned my head to see what was bringing him such joy. There in front of me was a group of animals with swinging trunks and giant feet. I heard Briden exclaim: "Elephants!"

Briden began to trot and I followed. Mosey followed us and before long we were among the biggest animals on earth. Orif was not far behind, delighting in the elephants as much as we were. Briden asked the largest one to spray him and without a second's hesitation, the elephant dipped his trunk into the river beneath the falls and sprayed Briden. The look of joy that came over my best friend's face was the best sight I had seen in many days. For a fleeting moment all thoughts of the wicked beast that ate camels was forgotten.

We romped and played, and before we knew it, the afternoon was ending and the signs of sunset were fast approaching.

Orif was worried. He said to us, "Oh my, we have stayed far too late. Your master and Sundar and the three kings are going to be angry with me. Ram will tan my hide. What are we to do? Soon it will be dark and there is no way we can make it back in the pitch of night."

The largest elephant stepped up to Orif and folded his front and back legs and was soon eye-level to the Sherpa. The elephant then waved his trunk and two of the other elephants kneeled like their leader.

The elephants motioned with their trunks for Orif and me to climb up on their backs before they stood up. The leader elephant had Briden take hold of his tail in his mouth and Mosey was made to hold onto a leather strap that Orif dangled from the elephant's back.

The elephants knew the path back to Pokhara in the darkness. Slowly, but surely, we lumbered through the moonlit meadows and mountain trails.

We finally arrived, and, I must say, we made quite a sight as we walked through the streets of the city. When we arrived at the King's palace, my master and Sundar were there to greet us. They had just set out with Ram to try and find us.

It was quite a reunion and the rest of that evening was spent with the elephants. They took my master and me for a ride around the city. Briden and Mosey walked along side us, and for that sweet moment; we were all happy and safe. The elephants stayed in the city that night and Briden and I snuck out of the palace courtyard to lay beside them until the sun rose over the highest peak.

That morning, the elephants took off for the elephant valley next to the falls, but before they left, the leader elephant took Briden and me aside. He said to us, "Beware of the red furred creature who inhabits the far side of the mountain south west of Pokhara." He paused and spoke again..., "I have to tell you he has a taste for camels and will stop at nothing to get you. When you make the pass through the mountain of which I speak, watch for patches of his fur on the rose brambles and the cry he makes during the day, which sounds like a camel braying in distress. This is how he baits his prey. Many other camels have fallen to sounds of the crying beast and have never returned from the mountain forest where he lives."

This news made Briden so fearful that he ran back to the palace courtyard.

Then the leader elephant turned to me and said, "Issa be steadfast and despite what Briden says, I think you must tell you master about the beast if the moment calls for it."

*****

The next morning we began our journey towards home, although home seemed like a far distant dream. My memories of Mary and Joseph and of course, Romey, made me anxious for our return. But I knew that the journey would be long…and the dangers many.

CHAPTER 4

Ram and the other Sherpas were busy packing the animals and gathering supplies for the journey home.

Briden and Mosey were pre-occupied with the preparation, so I was entirely on my own. My master was staying in the temple with Melchoir and the other wise men, so I decided to see what they were up to. I entered the main room of the temple, which was decorated with turquoise and moonstones. A massive rotunda capped the room and sunlight poured in from arched windows that measured twenty feet high.

I heard voices coming from a room connected to the big room, so I went closer. I recognized my master's voice and nudged the door open with my nose. My master and the three wise men were looking at a map of the sky.

I crept very quietly and hid behind a large chair that afforded me a very good view of the men.

Melchior spoke first, "The moment I saw the star, I consulted the map."

He pointed to a spot on the map before he continued, "We followed this star and it led to Bethlehem, and you. "

My master smiled.

Casper asked him, "Did you have a day when you knew you were different from the other children?"

Master thought for a moment and finally responded, "When I was eight or so, my cat, Mau, was stuck in a Terebinth tree near our home. He was crying and very frightened. I prayed the cat return safely to the ground, and suddenly, Mau floated downwards from the top of the tree to a sweet patch of clover below."

All three of the wise men loved the story and laughed heartily.

I, however, was far from amused. I had heard some of the rumors about Mau floating about town with Jesus by his side when I first moved in with my master. I chose to bury the rumors deep inside my head, like I would bury a good bone, but this was very difficult because Mau tried to make me jealous every day of my life.

I was still hiding behind the chair, feeling more and more jealous, when, before I knew what was happening, I started to lift off the floor. I floated above the large chair and through the air, until I was at eye level with my master.

I looked at him, and without hesitation, licked his nose. He always loved it when I licked him, so he laughed and then made me rise even higher. I rose up to the top of the ceiling. I was so high that Jesus and the wise men appeared very small. I was terrified.

Then my master said, "It's all right Issa, you will not fall."

And of course when my master spoke these words I felt as safe as if I had been in his arms. Then he spoke to me again, "Issa are you still green with envy?"

Since my master spoke the dog language, I told him I was sorry for being jealous of Mau, but that sometimes it just seemed that Mau got to do all the spectacular things like climb trees and sleep for hours on master's colorful straw mat.

The wise men were laughing as my master spun me round and round in nothing but air. They watched me twirl high above their heads. Finally, after the laughing subsided, my master lowered me to the floor. I was so happy to be on the ground, I decided I never needed to float in mid air again...all my green envy vanished as well.

I must say though, that when I trotted off to find Briden that afternoon, I possessed an extreme lightness in my step.

When I found Briden, he was laying down with a very sad look on his face. He forced a smile when he saw me approach. I sat down with him and told him about how Jesus had lifted me up into the air inside the temple and how peculiar it felt to float.

Briden reminded me: "Issa, don't you remember when we discovered Sundar in the cave floating above the ground?"

" Yes," I replied, "I do recall, but I dismissed it as a trick or a figment of our imaginations."

Briden said, "Issa, it is not a trick. It is called levitating and only men with enormous powers over their minds can have this skill. "

Looking back, my master did not seem at all baffled by Sundar's trick. In fact, my master never mentioned the discovery of Sundar as peculiar. I began to wonder what else I didn't know about my master. I reckoned that I had a lot to learn and decided to find Sundar who seemed to have an answer for everything. And, of course, aside from my master, Sundar was the only human being I had ever met that could speak the dog language.

I turned to Briden, "Come with me dear Briden, let us pay a visit to Sundar."

Briden declined, "Not right now Issa. I am too anxious about the mountain monster to engage in any polite conversations. I must brace myself for the journey ahead and devise some plan for my very survival."

I looked at my camel friend who for the first time since knowing him seemed worn and frail. He was not his usual self. He looked hollow in the cheek and seemed hardly able to muster the energy to stand.

He knew what I was thinking as I looked at him with much worry. He said, "Issa, fear paralyzes even the best of us. This fear of mine has taken over my bones as well as my very soul."

I left him to rest and I set out to find Sundar.

I found Sundar with the Sherpas, gathering and securing the supplies for our journey ahead. He asked, "Where is Briden?"

I explained to him that Briden was taking a nap.

Sundar's forehead furrowed and his eyebrows came way low over his black eyes. He asked me again, "What is wrong with Briden? Now tell me the truth. "

I hung my head and aimed my eyes to the ground for I knew that Sundar could smell a lie a mile away.

I said in a whisper, "He's fine. He is just resting up for the long journey ahead."

Sundar insisted I look at him and speak up. "Tell me the truth, Issa. What is happening with Briden?"

I spilled the whole story to Sundar. I told him about the monster and how Briden was scared witless about the journey ahead. I explained that he was so frightened he couldn't even get up.

I studied the expression on Sundar's face. The creases in his face grew deeper.

He turned to me and asked me, "Issa, do you believe that there is a monster that eats camels blood for good luck? "

The question threw me off guard because it never occurred to me not to believe the story. For a moment my hopes rose, maybe, just maybe, Sundar would tell me the monster story was just mountain myth and I could run to Briden and relieve his worst fears.

But instead, Sundar sighed a ragged sigh and said, after it seemed all the air inside him was gone, "Issa, it is true, I have heard these stories. I have never seen the monster myself, but the local mountain people swear there is such a creature. When we made the first leg of our journey without confrontation with the beast, I dismissed the notion as nonsense. But lately, I have heard the locals say that the monster comes around when there have been no rains, and there has been no rain since our arrival." He looked straight into my soul.

I looked back at him. "What are we going to do Sundar? "

He just said, "Let me think. Let me think. "

While Sundar was thinking, I decided to tell him about how my master floated me all the way to the top of the temple ceiling. That put a smile on his face. I pleaded with him, "Please Sundar, tell me about this power and tell me why my master is different from other men. And how are you different from ordinary men?"

Sundar replied, "Issa, I learned to levitate from many years of study. My mind can overcome normal doubt; my mind can overcome normal adversities; my mind is trained to deny ordinary physics and mathematics. I have been schooled in the art of transformation."

I repeated his phrase and asked, "The art of transformation? What is that?"

Sundar answered, "The ability to change, the ability to obstruct normal flows of energy and reverse them. It is the ability to bend and float and melt whatever needs to bend or float or melt." He paused and asked me, "Do you understand?"

I had to tell him the truth. I said to him, "No. I do not understand."

Sundar smiled and said, "It is not necessary to understand about me. I am a mere magician, a trickster. I am someone who plays with the dimensions, but does not necessarily understand them myself." He paused...,"...but your master...he is different from anyone that has been before him. Even the Great Buddha would agree with that...and even the Great Krishna would agree with that."

He picked up a crooked stick and began to draw in the dry earth. He drew a line and said to me, "Above the line is Heaven and below the line is earth. Your master

CHAPTER 4

understands the ways of both, for he is born from both places. He is from Heaven and he is from Earth. There has never been a human brought to us like *Him* before." He patted my head before asking me, "Do you understand? "

I looked up and asked him, "Does that make him God?"

Sundar looked at me and said, "Yes Issa, that makes your master God."

I left Sundar and walked some distance. I settled myself in a grove of pomegranate trees. I needed to think. Being a dog, I was not feeling completely equipped to comprehend the information that Sundar had revealed to me. I was in shock really and kept asking myself: "My master is God? My master is God?...but...Why me?"

As I lay in the pomegranate grove, I was suddenly overcome by a familiar odor. The odor caused my heart to pound and my fur to stand on end. My insides felt tight. I sprang up to my feet and began to growl and bark and spin around, looking for the source of the stench. I spun to my left only to have my worst fears realized. There, behind the largest tree in the grove, was my enemy. He was cloaked in a woolen robe that stank of a hideous mildew and small mushrooms and succulents were growing out of the knitted fabric. His face was not visible inside the hooded robe he wore.

The fur on my back rose even higher as I approached him. The closer I got, the more the earth underneath my feet began to shake. The stench was vile, and the tempest beneath me made movement near impossible.

My enemy lurched toward me, laughing in a hideous demonic fashion. As he approached me, he crouched, as if he were about to pounce on my head. I suddenly remembered the sensation of floating earlier in the day. I closed my eyes and wished for my body to float and, as if by magic, I lifted off the ground. When I was at the level of the tallest branches I observed my enemy's cloak fall to the ground and out from the woolen heap a viper slithered off and vanished.

I didn't want to stick around and think about what happened, I only wanted to get back to Briden as fast as I could. As luck would have it, Sundar and Briden were together. They took one look at me and knew something was terribly wrong.

Sundar stood up, his voice high pitched with concern, "Issa, what ghost have you seen?"

I answered, " It was no ghost. It was my enemy." I turned to Briden and lamented, "He has found me Briden."

Briden managed to muster a question for me. He asked, "Issa, my dear Issa, how did you escape?"

"I remember floating," I blurted out, "I levitated."

Briden was aghast and Sundar was pleased.

Briden's face was somber as he spoke, "I am happy for you, but I don't think I will have such good fortune when I run into the beast who wants to make mince of me. How is an animal like me supposed to levitate?"

Sundar spoke up, "Maybe we can teach you Briden. After all, my dear camel friend, being able to levitate is not a matter of physics; it is a matter of non-physics. We break the rules when we lift off. Don't you see?"

Briden did not want to see. He only wanted to dig himself deeper and deeper into despair.

I asked, "Why don't we practice...at least try," I begged.

So Sundar asked Briden to close his eyes, which he did, and then he asked Briden to imagine being a cloud floating effortlessly in the sky.

Sundar spoke in a whisper that became a lullaby of sorts. He whispered to Briden, "The clouds are above our heads and just as the clouds pass by without concern or anxiety for anything, you are now embodying the spirit of these clouds."

Briden was on his knees and I kept looking to see if he would lift even an inch off the ground. But try as Sundar did to get Briden to lift, he stayed as he was, heavy on the ground. He did not budge.

I began to chant: "You can fly. You can fly. You can fly."

But Briden remained in his earthbound posture, his knees folded underneath his body. His lips curled into a despairing grimace. He opened his eyes and spoke in a raspy manner. "It's no use, I am doomed to be captured by the beast. I am doomed to have my humps ripped off my back. The monster will drink my store of water and he will live on and I will die."

It was very hard to comfort him, because the likelihood of the monster getting him seemed reasonable. The season had been bone dry and this, we knew, was what made the monster crazy for camel blood.

At about that time we heard Ram calling out for us, "Sundar! Briden! Issa!"

His voice boomed across the city and made it's way to us on the outskirts. Ram was a man small of stature, but because he had climbed throughout the Himalayas his entire life, his capacity to inhale the mountain air and yell louder than any average man was staggering. He yelled again, "Sundar! Briden! Issa! It is time to go!"

I became excited. I wanted to get as far away from Pokhara as possible, especially now that my enemy was in the region. I reckoned that he would think twice about harassing me again, since I had shown such skill at intimidating him, but despite my victory over him, I was aiming to never see the likes of him again. So at the news of leaving, I became very happy. *Hurray! We are going home. Home to Mary and Joseph, home to Romey, and yes, even home to Mau the cat.* At last we would see the Terebinth trees, the olive groves and the sloping hills of Nazareth.

"Come on!" I cried to Sundar and Briden. But as I turned around to rouse them, my heart sank. Sundar was struggling to get Briden to his feet. The sight of my dearest friend, in his sorrowful and fearful state was almost too much to bear. Suddenly, I felt discouraged as I accompanied Sundar and Briden back into the city.

Ram was angry with us for not being ready. He was cursing under his breath, complaining that he would have to spend an hour outfitting Briden for the journey.

Briden was stoic as Ram packed both sides of his saddle with supplies. I refused to leave Briden's side despite Ram's efforts to shoo me away.

But Ram was insistent I make myself useful somewhere else. Sundar whistled to me and asked me to join him to make one last visit to the temple. I accepted the invitation and along the way Sundar told me that this would be the last time he saw his father.

He said, "Issa, I am destined to spend the rest of my life with you and your master. And because of this, I will not stay in India with my father. Despite the love I have for him, my path is clear. This is my destiny. It is in the stars."

I chose to remain silent, for I could only imagine how difficult it was going to be for Sundar to tell his father goodbye.

Melchior was studying in the same room where I had floated to the ceiling earlier that morning. I stood by Sundar as he told Melchior of his plans.

His father listened and said, "If I were a younger man I would be going with you as well."

I thought this was a wonderful idea, for Melchior to join us, I barked and ran in circles around the old man. He said to me, "Many years ago I came to your land to meet your master. I never expected to meet him as a young man. My fellow companions Caspar and Balthasar feel that we are twice blessed."

He looked at Sundar and took his hand. He said, "Go my son. I bestow my blessings on your journey."

They embraced, and I cried, for my heart ached for the old man.

As we were leaving, Melchior called out to us. He warned, "My son, beware of the beast that is said to lurk past the second valley."

I stopped dead in my tracks. Sundar asked his father if there was a weapon or a way to overcome him.

Melchior answered, "So far, nothing has been able to stop him. Use your wits; that is all I can suggest."

And with that, he went back into the vast library of the Pokhara temple.

On the way to the caravan, we met up with my master who was walking with Mosey.

My master was happy and very excited about the journey home. He told me just a few days earlier that he needed to get back and see his father and mother. "It is time," he said, "It's time to return home."

When all the goodbyes had been said, and the preparation was complete, we set out for our journey.

*****

The morning we left Pokhara the sun was shining and the breeze was saturated with the fragrance of rhododendron and rose.

Melchoir and Caspar waved goodbye until we were completely out of sight.

The first hours of the trip were festive. The Sherpas, even Ram, were singing and joking as I trotted from the front of the line to the back. I was determined to keep my eyes on Briden who was walking with Sundar. They had positioned themselves in the middle of the caravan line, figuring it would be the safest place to be.

At lunch time the caravan stopped in a beautiful valley. The trees were tall and blooming with giant white flowers. These flowers were so fragrant that they made us all feel a bit giddy. I decided to take a nap, so I lay next to Mosey, who was so tired she had already fallen asleep. I heard a caw, then a "caw caw." I looked up and saw an enormous raven-colored bird perched above my head. His eyes were black with a mustard-colored center, and as he stared, I could not resist the majesty and the determination of their gaze. I shook my body as I tried to unlock myself from the magnetism of his stare, but I was literally captured by his hold.

The only thing to do was bark, so that is what I did. I barked and barked and before long, Ram came running toward me. He scolded me, "Hush! Hush! This is our rest period you are waking everybody up."

Since Ram did not understand dog language there was nothing I could say to him, so I barked again and looked up at the tree where the bird was, and to my disappointment, the bird was gone. Two of his feathers floated down slowly from above and landed at my paws. I picked them up in my mouth and took them to Sundar.

Sundar examined them and determined that they were an omen about the second valley.

Sundar and I made our way to the middle of the line and joined Briden who was already up with his saddle fully packed. He seemed remote and all my attempts at light-hearted conversation fell flat. To make matters worse, the sun was blazing hot on that afternoon and there was not a cloud in the sky. Even the ground was parched and cracked, and most of the grass in the first meadow was a sun bleached yellow.

The Sherpas were alarmed. Jatta, one of the older Sherpas said to Ram,

"I have never seen such a dry season. Do you think we should travel around the second valley to avoid the beast?"

Of course, he had no idea that Briden and I could understand what he was saying. Sundar spoke up and asked, "Jatta, what are you talking about? Is there some danger in the second valley that we need to know about?"

Jatta started to speak, but Ram interrupted him before he had a chance to say a word. Ram said, "There is no danger in the second valley, only myths and hearsay that give me a headache. Jatta is a fool; don't listen to him."

I growled at Ram. I wanted to bite him. Every instinct in my body saw him as a cruel and evil man that needed to be taught a lesson. Sundar hushed me and held me back. He asked Ram, "My dear Ram, I hope that you are not leading our caravan into danger, for if you are, and one of our lives are lost, you will be facing a life of very grave karmic consequences."

Sundar paused and stared deeply into Ram's black sunken eyes.

Ram stared back and yelled at the top of his voice, "Move south. Second valley!"

And with that, the front of the line shifted directions and the caravan set out for the second valley, which we were to reach by the next day.

The youngest Sherpa, Pi, and his wife Lata were traveling close to my master and Mosey. Pi and Lata were the cooks and were also very fond of my master, as was everyone. Master was fond of the couple because they laughed so easily and made him laugh as well.

When we set up camp for the night, Pi and Lata put a pot on to boil. They filled it with rice and fresh spices, and the aroma from the dish made everyone in the camp happy, for we all knew a good meal was ahead.

My master was always curious and decided to explore the last bit of the first valley. I asked him, "Master, do you want me to join you?"

He answered, "That is fine of you to ask Issa, but why don't you stay here with Briden? He needs your company very much."

I wanted to tell master how much I was afraid for Briden and how I thought that Ram was leading us into a death trap for my friend, but I didn't. I remained silent, for I had promised Briden not to say a word.

Still my master asked me, "Issa, do you have something you wish to say to me?"

I lied and said, "Nothing, master. Nothing at all."

That night, Lata and Pi prepared a delicious meal that pleased everyone. Master was with Mosey toward the front of the camp where one of the Sherpas was telling stories about his many travels in the Himalayas.

Sundar had settled in with some of the other Sherpas on the edge of the camp. They were drinking a rice beer that was making them very drunk. The sounds of their merrymaking could be heard while the rest of the camp was preparing for a good night's sleep.

Before I went to where Briden was resting, I found Sundar with the men. I asked him, "Sundar will you please come to Briden and me soon?"

He answered, "Don't worry Issa; I will come soon. You and Briden have nothing to fear."

I thanked him and said, "Briden and I are relying on you to stand guard and I can take over when you need to sleep."

I was pleased that Sundar had promised to come soon, but as I started to trot off toward Briden, one of the Sherpas asked me if I had ever tasted rice beer. Of course he didn't know I could understand him, so all the other men, including Sundar, started laughing.

Sundar said to the men, "You better be careful, because this dogs understands our language."

They laughed at Sundar for being a fool. One of the men said, "You are crazy to think a dog can understand us."

Sundar defended his honor and said, "No I am sure of it. Issa speaks and understands."

That just made the men more sarcastic.

I decided, right then, that I had to prove to these men that Sundar was right. So, with great swagger, I walked over to the bowl of rice beer and drank.

To my surprise, it had a most pleasant taste and before long it produced a very desirable state of relaxation. I was delighted to be free of my worries, so I kept drinking the rice beer.

Soon Sundar and I began to entertain the men. Sundar would give me a command and I would perform the command. If Sundar said, Issa bark four times, I would bark four times. The men were amazed by my intelligence. The more they laughed and applauded, the more I wanted to entertain them. Sundar and I were, by now, rather drunk, and before long, we lost our wits. Sundar passed out, and because my head was spinning, I decided to close my eyes for just a moment.

*****

When I awoke my head was splitting, and for a second I did not even know where I was. Sundar was still sleeping and I shook him to wake him up. The sun was just rising over the mountains. I said, "Sundar wake up; we need to get back to Briden!"

Sundar opened his eyes and jumped up. " Come on," he said, and we ran as fast as we could back to camp.

My heart was beating so fast as the dread in my heart was almost unbearable. When we arrived to our place in the line, there was no Briden. I felt the blood run out of my body, a weakness took hold of me as I frantically scattered about to see if Briden might be behind a tree or hiding under a carpet.

But he was nowhere and Sundar began yelling for our dear friend at the top of his lungs, "Briden! Briden! Where are you?"

By this time, the camp was waking up and scrambling about, asking us where the camel had gone. Soon my master showed up with Mosey by his side. He asked me, "Issa, where is Briden? Were you and Sundar not guarding your friend?"

This was the worst moment of my life, because I had to tell my master that I had failed and betrayed my friend. I had to tell him that I was drunk with a band of men, including Sundar, and that we had slept through the night in a drunken haze.

I saw Ram running towards us. He looked furious and ready to start trouble. He was screaming, "What is the hold up? Where is the big camel?"

Sundar spoke up, "Ram, he is gone." Sundar was sobbing by now. He went on, "Issa and I have failed and now the monster has grabbed him."

Sundar fell to his knees with his head buried in his hands.

My master knelt beside the distraught Sundar and asked him, "Sundar, what do you mean by monster? Are you speaking the truth?"

Ram interrupted and said to Sundar, "You fool. There is no monster. Maybe the camel ran back to Pokhara because he is a coward. That is more like it. And he has my supplies on his back! Now what am I going to do?"

Ram made me so mad I growled and showed my fangs. I was just about to jump on his wicked head, but master held me back.

Jesus scolded Ram, "How dare you say such things about the brave and good Briden. He is our friend and I hope you will help us find him."

I looked up at master and spoke my fastest, I told him, "No master, Ram knows about the monster but he does not care about Briden's safety. The monster is only after camels because of the drought. He rips off their humps to save the water inside. It is good luck to eat the camel's blood, and the humps give him long-life."

I was out of breath when I finished and master looked at me like I was still drunk. Then he looked at Sundar, who was still on his knees. Sundar spoke up for me and said, "Dear Jesus, your dog Issa is telling the truth. This is what we have heard and even my father, the wise Melchior, warned us about the beast."

Jesus asked, "What did your father say? How did he suggest we find the beast?"

Sundar's head lowered. He said to Jesus, "He did not say how to find him. He only said to use our wits."

Suddenly we heard loud caws over our heads. It was the black bird that I had seen the day before. He was diving over my head and screeching. I knew he was saying, follow me; follow me. While everyone made plans to find Briden, I took off after the black bird.

I must have chased after the bird for at least two miles because when I could not run another step, I looked around and knew we were in the second valley. It was very quiet, as if no living things were around. By now, the black bird was hopping in front of me. I followed his delicate hops and soon I was standing in front of the entrance to a dark mountainous cave. I barked and howled and growled to get the beasts attention.

As I was barking, I began to feel the earth shake beneath my legs. A dark shadow behind me was making it more and more difficult to see into the cave entrance. Finally, it occurred to me to stop barking into the cave and turn around.

I felt the blood leave my body. Never have I seen such a horrid creature, Never could I have imagined such a beast. But there he was towering before me, like a mountain of fierce evil. He was covered in reddish fur and his paws were bigger than the whole of me. I was trembling so much I was unable to move. Somehow I managed a scream, "Where is my friend?"

The monster reared his head and laughed. He pointed inside the cave and said, "He is mine. I need his special water to survive. Only rainwater fresh from the sky is as good as a camel's water." His voice was thunderously low. He bent down and tried to grab me. He said, "I like dog for supper."

I ran between the monsters legs and jumped on his back. My teeth sank into his fur. I held on for dear life as he twisted back and forth to shake me off his back. I thought briefly about my enemy and how I had levitated to escape, but if I went higher in this case, the monster could strike me down with one swipe of his paw. I started praying, "Oh Master, look at me now, if you are God, can you save me and can you save my dear friend Briden?"

The second after I uttered my prayer, I felt a drop of water hit my head. Within a few more seconds the sky turned a purplish black and thunder and lightning threatened the entire second valley.

With the sky opening up, and the crash of thunder all about, the monster stopped thrashing about. He stood still and suddenly I was dangling from his backside, my teeth clinched into his thick red fur.

Then the rain came. At first it was slow with big droplets hitting my head, but it did not take long for the slow fat droplets to turn into a mighty downpour.

The monster lifted his arms towards heaven and started jumping and dancing with me on his back. His dry fur became soaked and soon I was sliding off his back and down his leg and on to the ground. The monster was laughing and dancing. He picked me up and kissed me on the head, right between my eyes. He said, "You are my miracle. You have brought rain to my valley!"

He was bouncing me as a father bounces his newborn son. He was smothering me in kisses and singing a song about the rain. I managed to speak in between the bounces, "Oh please, Monster, can you take me to Briden now?"

He answered, "I will take you to my cave."

The roar of the rain was deafening as we made our way to the cave. We entered the blackness. The monster stopped after a short distance and put me down. He stoked a fire so that I could see and asked me to wait. I stood still by the fire as the monster went deeper inside.

On the sides of the walls were many drawings of every kind of camel that could be thought of. Double humped camels, single humped camels, camels with saddles on their back and others that were without saddles. I shuttered at the thought of so many camels that had lost their lives to the beast.

I began to worry that the monster would not return with Briden and just as I decided to go deeper into the cave to check on Briden, I could see a faint shadow of something coming out of the dark. To my dismay, it was my dearest friend Briden walking toward me with the beast behind him. I ran to Briden and began to cry and apologize for letting him down. I cried to him, "Oh Briden, will you ever be able to forgive me? Will you ever be able to forgive Sundar and me for letting you down?"

Briden was so happy to be alive that he forgave me straight away.

He said, "Issa, we all fail and we all make mistakes. You are my best friend and you saved me!"

By now the monster was seated beside us and he spoke in a tone that did not seem monster like at all. He explained, "For many centuries my ancestors have had to survive in the second valley, which is the only valley in all of the Himalayas that never gets rain. We learned very early that camels have water in their backs and that is what made us terrorize your kind for so long."

The monster leaned in closer to Briden, who had a very sad look on his face. Briden asked the monster, "Why can't you drink from the streams?"

The monster said, "It is only fresh rain water or the water from a camel's hump that gives us strength. I am a dying breed and so far, no one has ever understood our peculiar set of difficulties. Everyone calls us monsters or beasts, so that is what we became, only to survive."

The monster hung his horrid head and looked as sad as anything or anyone I have ever seen before or since. Before we had a chance to continue, the black bird that led me to the cave flew in with my master and Sundar behind him.

I ran to master and jumped in his arms. I exclaimed, "Oh Master, Briden was saved. I made a miracle of rain!"

Jesus asked me how I did such a wondrous thing. I replied, "I prayed."

He asked me, "And who do you think listened?"

Before I had a chance to ponder the question and respond Sundar and Briden were hugging each other. The monster stood silently by. He looked sad.

My master embraced him. It must have been the first time that anyone had ever held him and loved him, because he began to cry like a baby.

My master stepped back and said to the monster, "From here on out there will always be plenty of rain in your valley. You will never have the blood of any camel on your paws. You are free from being called a monster and will forever more be thought of as the gentle creature of the second valley."

The creature was filled with joy.

Briden thanked the black bird that was sitting on the creature's furry head. As we were saying our goodbyes, Sundar got on top of Briden's back with me in his arms.

My master planned to walk beside us, but Briden told him he felt strong enough to carry us all. We began our trek back to camp, but before we could get two trots away, the creature warned us to beware of Ram.

The monster said, "Ram is an evil man."

My master thanked the creature for the warning, but as we traveled back, we knew more danger lay ahead.

CHAPTER 5

A mile or so out from camp, Sundar yelled over the torrential rains, "I am so hungry that I can hardly wait to see what Pi and Lata have prepared for lunch."

I began to imagine rice and dried fish with hot bread. Lata, the cook's wife, made sure to wake up early every morning to prepare stacks of the nan bread, and Pi made sure we had plenty of Indian butter, called ghee, and honey.

Even my master was imagining what delicacies awaited us. He said, "Maybe Pi will have made the apricot bread with almonds."

With the mention of the sumptuous meal that awaited us, Briden picked up the pace.

Sundar sang, "Pi makes the cake, Lata makes the bread, before too long, we will all be fed. La la la la la la la la la la la."

Soon we were all singing the silly song.

We weren't far from camp when the rain suddenly stopped. There were no sounds coming from the direction of our camp, nor were there any delicious aromas from the cook's pot. Sundar hopped off Briden's back and began to run towards the camp.

Briden ran after him with my master and me holding on for dear life. Suddenly, Briden stopped dead in his tracks.

It was Pi lying in a pool of his own blood, his head torn off and askew to one side. Lata was kneeling beside him, wailing like a child. Her colorful yellow sari splattered with her husband's blood.

I rubbed my eyes. I thought it must be a bad dream or a figment of my imagination. My master and I leapt off Briden's back, carried by what could have only been a supernatural strength. My master went to Lata; she would not let go of Pi's lifeless body.

Sundar went to Pi's head and collapsed with despair. He cried, "Pi, my friend, I have known you since you were a boy. My father helped raise you, and now look at you." Then he screamed and shook his fists at the heavens. "Why? Why? Who could have done such an act?"

I had never seen a severed head. I wanted to smell the blood, but Sundar screamed at me to stop. I ran under Briden's long legs, but Briden yelled out at me as well. He said, "How can you go after the blood of our dear Pi? Are you a monster too?"

I ignored them and started barking at the blood and the gore. I wanted my barking to put it all back together as it was before we left. I hopped and ran in circles howling and twirling until I was dizzy with my own madness. I ran up to my master and licked his face and licked Lata's blood splattered arm. It tasted sweet. It tasted like Pi. I barked again. Master shushed me away. He was very pale.

Finally, I could only lie beside Lata and cry with her. I whimpered until my throat ached. I stayed next to her for some time not aware that other things were going on around me. Sundar had taken Pi's head and washed it with rose water. He set Pi's head down as he emptied out a bag that Lata had filled with turnips the day before. He shook the contents of the bag free. Turnips were rolling around all over the ground. He then placed Pi's head inside the cotton bag.

Sundar hoisted the bag over his shoulder and yelled, "Ram where are you? Ram! Ram!"

There was dead silence...and then a swish from behind some huge rhododendron trees. I ran as fast as I could and looked up. My vision was different. I could see little scales and fine hairs underneath the leaves and the flowers were steaming with a heady fragrance. I felt dizzy.

I looked behind the trunk of the tree closest to me. There was the youngest Sherpa with two of his brothers. They were shaking and fell to the ground when they saw Sundar behind me. They began to speak in a strange dialect that I could not understand. Sundar was screaming at them, "What happened here? Where is Ram?"

They were crying. Tears were rolling down their once pink cheeks.

"He took the donkey named Mosey and…"

The one crying the most pointed to the north, "…that's all we know," he said.

In the calamity, I had not noticed that Mosey was gone. I did not believe them at first. I ran to look for her. Sundar was calling me, but I paid no mind. I had to find her, but she was not in any of the places where I looked. I found master, still with the grieving Lata and explained to him that Ram had taken off with Mosey.

Lata spoke for the first time. She said, "They went to the home of his ancestors…." She paused…then went on…"Ram went mad with anger when it began to rain. He was screaming: 'They have broken the spell! They have broken the spell!' Pi went to comfort Ram, as it looked like the devil had taken over his mind, and that is when…"

Lata began to shake, tears were rolling down her face, now the color of a magnolia petal. She continued, "That is when he lobbed off Pi's head with his mighty sword and grabbed the little donkey. He jumped on Mosey's back, swatted her flanks and rode towards Jimpur, his home village." At that, Lata started sobbing again.

Master and I wasted no time. Master asked, "Where is Jimpur? "

Lata answered, "It is north of the second valley."

Master, Briden, Sundar and I wasted no time. We left one of the Sherpas with Lata and took one with us and set out for the second valley. Our path was still fresh from earlier in the day, so we followed it with ease.

It had not been an hour earlier that we had been singing silly songs and looking forward to a good meal. I couldn't help thinking about Pi's head laying cold in a cotton turnip bag and that we were going back to the valley again. The rain had let up, but the forest and valley beyond were a vibrant green and the air smelled of fresh rain. It was not long before the beast of the second valley caught our scent and found us not far from the village of Jimpur.

He was startled to see us and asked, "What brings you back to my valley? Did you miss me that much?" He laughed as he thought that was very funny.
He could immediately tell by the distraught looks on our faces that something terrible had happened. He asked, this time with much concern, "What is the trouble that I see on your faces?"

Sundar spoke, "When we returned to our camp we found our cook brutally murdered. His head was cut off and we believe that Ram was the evil doer."

Sundar asked the beast, "Do you know of him and his family? Do they live in the village of Jimpur?"

The beast let out a great sigh that smelled of green leaves. He explained,

"Ram and his family are the ones that put a curse on this valley and on me. They have dark magic and believe that the blood of camels will bring them good luck and power."

Briden winced when the beast said this. The beast went on, "When you made it rain, the curse was lifted. Ram went mad for fear of losing his power, as well as knowing that his family would, most likely, fall into shame." He paused and went on, "The other villagers hate Ram and his family."

Briden asked, "Where can we find him? He has taken our dear Mosey. We must now rescue her, for Mosey is an animal of destiny."

Briden hung his head and started to sniffle with emotion.

I immediately said, "Briden, dear friend, it is no time for tears now. We must rescue Mosey."

I spied Mosey and started barking. Sundar hushed me and made Briden kneel, as we approached the village.

Just outside Jimpur Jesus stopped and spoke in a whisper, "Sundar, you stay here with Briden. Issa and I will enter the village."

Mosey was tied up and looking very bedraggled. Ram had piled up mountains of gear on her back and she was baying with a sad hoarseness in her throat. She looked up and saw us. Her eyes lit up. "Hee Haw. Hee Haw." Mosey could not contain herself. "Hee Haw. He Haw," she bayed again.

I ran toward Mosey and suddenly felt a heavy object hit my head. I fell. That's all I remember.

I learned later that Ram had clobbered me on the head and that Jesus lifted Mosey and me up with the power of his mind and we floated back to where Briden and Sundar were crouched in the tall foliage that surrounded the village.

Briden said that Jesus entered the small hut-like structure and found Ram's family: all dead. There was evidence of a poisonous brew on the table. Then, Briden said, "Ram stumbled into the hut clearly planning on killing your master."

I shook with horror at such a notion.

"But before Ram had a chance, he fell dead on the floor. That's when Mosey ran to the hut and looked in. According to Mosey there was a frothy white substance coming from Ram's mouth and his eyes bulged and his legs shook."

"What next, I asked? "

" Slowly, but surely, the villagers came out of their huts and jumped for joy, knowing that Ram and his family were done with. Your master made sure the villagers buried the family and said prayers for their souls...."

Mosey interrupted Briden and continued with the story, "When we returned to the camp, Jesus laid you down and rested beside you. He petted your head and wetted you lips with water. Not long after that, Jesus moved you into Lata's tent. I followed to keep my eyes on you. After a short while, you began to make growling sounds in your sleep."

What I never told anyone was that I was dreaming about ripping Ram's head off with my teeth. I tore him to shreds and told him he would perish in hell and never be able to escape. I could not understand how Jesus had been able to allow Ram and his family to be buried properly and then to have prayers said for their souls.

When I finally woke up from my dream, I opened my eyes. Lata was still asleep next to me. I scooted close beside her and she brought me even closer with her arms. Her arms were warm and I knew that somewhere Pi was cold and dead. I hated Ram with all my heart. I decided his blood would taste like dessert: sweet and warm. I knew I would never taste Pi's warm ghee on Lata's nan bread ever again. I hated him for that alone. And poor Lata would never hold Pi again in her sleep and whisper precious words of love in his ears.

His ears were dead to the world. He would never sing again or make us laugh. He was cold and dead and his head was rotting inside a turnip bag. It was the smell of turnips and rot that finally woke me again. I was angry and set out to find my master.

I stood up carefully so not wake Lata. I made out the silhouette of Jesus in the early dawn light. He was resting beside Briden and Mosey. Mosey was asleep and Jesus was petting her gently.

I approached and nuzzled him to pay attention to me. He turned to me and smiled, "Dear Issa, I am so glad you are recovered." He petted my head.

It was always hard to be upset with my master for too long, but I went ahead and asked him the question that was burning into my heart, "Master, how could you have allowed Ram to have a proper burial and have prayers said for his soul? He killed our beloved Pi…and now Lata is alone." I started to cry.

He drew me close and held my head in his hands. He looked deeply into my tear-filled eyes. "Issa, it is always better to forgive. Hatred and anger do nothing for the rest of us. When we forgive, the world is healed…." He paused, and then went on. "…That is why we forgive. It is how we heal."

I looked straight at him and said, "I don't want to forgive Ram. I want to hate him."

Jesus said to me, "Issa I too understand how difficult it is to forgive...." He paused and continued. "Issa, ...just think on it. "

I walked away and found a spot to think, a good distance from the rest of the camp. I nestled under a lush flowering bush and closed my eyes. I had barely a moment of repose before I remembered a verse from the Old Book back home: *An eye for an eye, a tooth for a tooth.* That was something the old rabbi's had said that God had said. "How could God be wrong?" I asked myself. I was feeling pleased that my argument was beginning to take form.

A sound from around the bush distracted me for a moment and then what seemed to be an apparition became very real. The most beautiful dog I had ever seen, next to Romey of course, walked straight up to me. She sniffed my head and then sniffed my back. She introduced herself, "Hello, I am Mayse and I am very lost."

I bolted straight up and said, "I am Issa. Perhaps I can help you find your way."

She asked me where I came from and what I was doing out in the middle of nowhere alone.

I told her, "I am not alone, just taking a break from the others as I had to figure some things out."

"Like what?" she asked.

I broke down and told her the whole mess of the last day.

She listened attentively. She moved in close to me.

I smelled her fur and it smelled of fresh mountain air. Her eyelashes were long and they batted slowly over her perfectly shaped hazel eyes. She was beautiful and she kept sniffing my head and licking my left ear that was still sore from the pounding Ram gave it earlier.

"Does it still hurt? " she asked.

I replied, "Yes it does, but I am lucky enough to be alive from the ordeal."

She agreed and said to me, "I think your master, this Jesus, owes you an apology. You lost your friend Pi and this evil Ram tried to kill you too. You must go back to the village and dig up his grave and retrieve his head."

"Really? You think that is what I should do?"

She answered, "Oh yes. I know you are brave and you must avenge Pi's death for the sake of his widow Lata."

I asked her, "But what about my master telling me to forgive? "

Mayse said, "Forgiving is for cowards not for the stout of heart and brave of spirit."

I asked her, "You think I am brave?"

"Oh I can tell. You are the bravest dog I have ever met."

"I don't think I'm brave."

Mayse responded, "You can prove your bravery to me by taking me to Jimpur and defying your master. He is making you feel bad about having feelings of anger and hatred, and this is not right. Sometimes anger and revenge are the things that heal our souls." She paused and moved in closer. She started licking my ear again and then whispered most sweetly, "I will join you and together we will avenge the death of Pi by never forgiving Ram. We will dig up his bones and have a delicious meal. You can bring the head of Ram back to the widow."

She turned her face toward me very close and licked my nose. Without a moment's hesitation I agreed to the mission.

I was filled with pride to be along side such a beauty as Mayse, and not only that, but to be on my way to avenge the death of my friend Pi. I had thoughts of digging up Ram's head and trotting proudly back to Lata and showing her the trophy of revenge.

I could imagine Lata dropping to her knees and all the people of the camp praising me for my bravery and my honor and restoring justice to Lata. Sundar would take the head of Ram and tie it to a wooden stick and we would watch it shrink and shrivel all the way back home to Galilee. I would be a hero and ride on Mosey's back into

Nazareth, the city of our birth. Everyone would praise my name:

"Issa. Issa. The great dog Issa."

I would be humble and yet kingly in my manner, and the shrunken head of Ram would stand for courage and daring and seeking justice in an unjust world.

I was deep into my daydream, yet keenly aware of the lovely Mayse beside me. I felt drunk with power and glory.

"You are such a very handsome dog," she said.

We stopped and gazed into each other's eyes and it hit me. At first it was subtle and then more pungent. It was the undeniable odor of my enemy.

Mayse grew alarmed, "What? What is wrong? We do not have time to smell the roses, we have a mission to accomplish."

I sniffed the ground around us. I sniffed the tree to the left and the bush to the right and could not pin point where the stench was coming from. I blinked as if waking from a dream and smelled Mayse again. I jumped back from the stink of sulphuric rot rising from her perfect soft fur.

I felt the sting of betrayal and the flush of deceit as sure as if a hive of honeybees had covered me from head to tail. I felt on fire and my fur was emitting the same horrid odor of my enemy.

Instead of revulsion, I was curiously overcome with a sense of wicked pleasure. I became willing to do the worst things to keep the beautiful creature before me. Mayse wanted me and needed me to protect her. Therefore, I had to carry out the grave robbing ceremony so she would know I was the right partner for her. I decided I wanted to impress her at whatever cost.

I lied, "It's nothing. I just thought I heard something."

"Like what? You seem frail and weak suddenly."

"Me weak? Me frail? " I held my breath and licked her cheek. "Let's go."

We finally arrived at Jimpur. It was empty of people and empty of any signs of life. I concluded that the villagers were harvesting turnips. I trotted around looking for fresh graves.

Without much effort, I found the mounds of earth that promised the trophy of Ram's head.

Mayse stood beside me, "Well what are you waiting for? " She pushed me toward the mound.

"Get going. I am hungry and need some juicy meat to satisfy my hunger."

It occurred to me that I was hungry and needed food for the journey back to camp. *My triumphant journey back*, I thought as I began to dig. I rounded my spine and prepared for the hard work. Digging was a hard job, but that didn't matter at the time. All I had to do was look up at the stunning sight of Mayse basking in the late afternoon sun and the mere sight of her gave me all the energy I needed. I barked up at her, "Look at me. See what a brave dog I am."

She barked back with the softest most sensual promise of love.

I put aside the odor I smelled earlier. I convinced myself that I had imagined it and that I had totally misjudged the moment. I dug for an hour and to my horror came across a stack of bones. They were not new bones, but old and dried bones. They were not the bones of people. I picked up a large jawbone and thought it bore a resemblance to someone I knew.

That's when it struck me. It was a camel's scull. I looked deeper into the vast hole I had created and saw before me a large catacomb filled to the brim with the bones of camels. I noticed some steps leading down to another room. There were hundreds of bones and strange drawings on the inside of the crypt. Camels— and men killing camels—and camels falling—and their sweet blood being collected in golden cups. I saw the very same golden cups on the floor of the room stained with the dark remnants of old blood.

I yelped and ran with my tail tucked between my legs, only thinking of how it could have been my friend Briden rotting in the cold dark place of horror.

At the top of the stairs I bumped into Mayse. I warned her, "We must leave this place! We must go! This is the house of the devil himself."

But instead of Mayse budging or being alarmed by my assessment of the mass grave, she stood firm and growled at me. Her teeth were bared with a cruelty that shook my very soul.

"Move girl, move!" I screamed.

Mayse was firm and resolute at the top of the stairs. She would not let me get on one side or the other. She pushed me backwards and I tumbled down the stairs of the crypt. I hit my head slightly and felt the same wooziness that I had felt earlier in the day. I could not move. I was paralyzed with fear. I tried to stand upright but could not manage at all. Mayse came closer and closer.

I shrunk back as best I could. I knocked over some camel bones and a skull came crashing down on me. It hit my nose and I wailed with agony. I pleaded, "Please help me Mayse. We must get out of here."

Her lips curled up and her beautiful black nose rippled with layers of hideous flesh. The teeth in her head grew longer, until they practically reached to the floor. She growled and hissed at me, and then her wretched odor became profoundly noxious.

I was close to fainting or dying, for now I knew it was him or her, my enemy's faceless ambiguous shape rising up before me, poised to strike.

"You fool." The beautiful Mayse was laughing. She said, "Pray to your master now. Summon him back to the village. If he is go great he will save you."

Every instinct in my bones wanted to cry out to my master and plead for mercy, plead for help and rescue, but I knew if I did, my master would come and be in grave danger. I made myself think of other things other than my precious friend and master Jesus.

I thought of flowers in Tibet; I thought of mountain streams and small golden fish; I thought of the great elephants I met and the precious children in the city we had just left. I thought of the sun...and the rain that had fallen to save Briden...and it was then that I felt a palpable truth: that all things of beauty and goodness were the things of my master. And just thinking about these beautiful things was almost the same as praying. I decided to stare her down for she was the opposite of everything my master stood for.

"It won't work fool," she screamed. Then Mayse lunged for my throat.

Suddenly, a shaft of light hit the floor of the crypt. I looked up and saw Briden and Mosey with my master in between them.

Jesus raised his arms and Mayse flew backwards up the stairs. She hit the ground and her body split up into ten or twelve dogs. These dogs were no longer soft with curly fur; now they were spiked with the hair of wild boar. Briden and Mosey ran into the crypt and Briden recognized his ancestor's bones at once. He screamed and Mosey trembled.

I heard my master cry out to Mayse, "You cannot win! Be off with you!"

Suddenly, a shadow came over the entrance to the crypt. The shadow was cast from the mountain beast. He stood next to my master and together they blew with all their might. Their collective breath became a wind that twisted and shook the very earth. Briden and Mosey and I held on for dear life. The wind turned the sky black and as I looked up: I could see the hellhounds fly into the eye of the storm.

We heard their cries and saw their bones splay and break. But just before they disappeared, I saw the vision of Mayse, as she was, hauntingly beautiful. I shook my head and she was gone.

I was very quiet the whole way back to camp. My head hung low with great shame. I waited for my master to scold me. He kept silent. I thought about how Briden was able to forgive the mountain beast, and how Mosey was able to forgive me for getting us in such a mess. I was weary from all the thinking.

It was late when we arrived at camp. Everyone was asleep except Sundar who greeted us and gave us water and some dried fish to eat.

Master found a place to rest and I watched him from a distance. I looked at him and wondered how long it would be before he could forgive me. I eventually moved in closer and closer. He was breathing slow and even. There was a robe close to his feet and I pulled it over him. The night air was getting very cold. I scooted closer and whispered, "Master, I am so sorry for disobeying you. I hope you can one day forgive me for what I have done." I was sad to the very bottom of my soul and began to whimper.

He woke up. He took me in his arms and held me close. "Issa, we are all tempted to do wrong…." He paused as he petted my head. "I love you and forgive you completely."

I could not pretend to understand the message of forgiveness completely. The subject baffled me. I knew that I was glad Ram was dead and that Mayse was gone. I was not sure how or where to start forgiving, I just knew it felt extremely wonderful to have someone forgive me. So when sleep finally came and I was safe in my master's arms, I decided I had a whole lifetime to figure it out.

CHAPTER 6

It took us many months, almost a full year, before we arrived home. Galilee was a sight for sore eyes. The fragrance of the olive groves and the great Terebinth trees made everybody happy. The best surprise for me was that Romey was waiting for me. She was wagging her tail in my master's front doorway.

Romey moved in with us right away. Sundar, Briden and Mosey settled in the hills close by.

Master was happy to get back to his carpentry, and I was glad that we could at last settle down and live a normal life. I was hoping that we would never leave again. I was secretly imagining that my master would meet a woman and have children like I was planning to do with my dearest Romey.

I would daydream while my master and Joseph worked. I loved the smell of freshly cut pine and cedar, and indeed it did remind me of the earliest days of my youth. Life was finally back to how it should be; quiet, happy and safe. Then early one morning, my master woke me up and asked me to join him on a short trip into the desert.

I loved to go running and walking and chasing sticks with my master, especially when Romey joined us. Very often we would visit Briden, Sundar and Mosey, and we would fill Romey's head with stories about India. But on this early morning occasion, my master insisted that we stay quiet. Therefore, it was just the two of us that set out towards the great wilderness.

Even though I loved when Romey joined us, I was feeling jubilant and carefree that my master chose me, and me alone, for company. "Ha, look at me! My master, Jesus, chooses my company over that of man, woman, child, dog or beast!" I was running in circles, chasing squirrels and muskrats, sniffing at the wildflowers, barking at the prickly plants. I was oblivious for a short time, not noticing how much further we had gone than usual.

The ground was getting rougher and Nazareth was out of view. I looked around and heard a man yelling, "Repent, for the Kingdom of Heaven is at hand. I am the voice of one crying in the wilderness. Prepare the way of the Lord." The same voice cried this chant over and over again. We followed the voice and ended up cresting a small hill and ran right into this man crying out in the wilderness.

I saw him and started growling. He looked like a wild animal. He had a beard down to his waist and hair almost as long. He was dirty and tangled looking. He was standing on the banks of the river Jordon. There were fifteen or twenty people around him listening to him cry out.

I could not help myself. I ran towards this odd man and started barking and trying to get at the cloak of animal fur he had draped over his shoulders. It didn't take long for Jesus to catch up and gently reprimand me for behaving so badly. "Calm down Issa. I must speak with this man," he said, firmly.

Reluctantly, I stopped growling.

But instead of speaking to one another, they looked at one another for a very long time. Then a very strange thing happened: The stranger cloaked in fur walked into the water. The day was calm and the sky was very blue. Suddenly, some doves flew back and forth overhead.

My master then stepped down into the water with this man and said, "John the Baptist I am ready."

I immediately followed my master into the water. It felt cool and refreshing. I stood as close to my master as possible as it was a bit hard to keep my balance from the fast currents that ran through the Jordan.

This stranger, who my master now called by name asked, "I am the one who needs to be baptized by you. Why do you come to me? "

I was amazed because I was thinking the exact same thing: *Yes, Master, why do you come to him? This ragamuffin of a man?*

Master looked down to me and I knew to hold my tongue. Then my master said to John the Baptist, "Let it be this way. You baptize me, for it is fitting thus to fulfill all righteousness."

And before I knew it, the stranger poured water from the river on my master's head and some of that water dripped onto my head too. Within a second of time, a beautiful white dove appeared above our heads and the clouds whirled and swirled and came down over us, yet the sun still shone bright as ever. Both my master and the stranger looked up at the sky as if they were hearing something that I could not hear.

We left very soon after this strange event. My master bowed his head as we walked quickly away. I spoke to him after some time, "Master, it is going to be late soon. Perhaps we should return to Nazareth. You're parents might worry, and Romey will be concerned as well."

He replied, "Issa, I must keep walking into the wilderness to pray and fast. My father has instructed me to stay for forty days and forty nights before I can begin my ministry."

I ran around him in circles. I implored, "How could you hear Joseph all this way off? I didn't hear your father say anything about forty days and forty nights!"

My master remained patient and said in a whisper, "Not my earthly father Issa, my heavenly father."

I was sad for the first time since our return home. I had Romey to look after, especially since I found out that she was carrying our pups in her belly. I looked up at him and knew that he understood everything I was thinking.

"Issa, I understand that you must go back to Nazareth. Please know that you have my blessing to leave, so run with the wind and let our family know what has happened."

I left him alone on a bluff. The sun was setting and the pink sky blazed behind my master as I tore off into the night. I looked behind as I ran, until he became a silhouette, standing alone, watching me disappear into the dunes.

I ran and ran until I reached our home. Romey was so glad to see me she ran in circles and jumped up and down. When she settled down, I told her about what had happened.

After she listened to the whole story, she said, "Issa, you must go and protect your master."

I could not believe what I was hearing from her. I was hurt. I spoke firmly to her and said, "No Romey, I must stay with you and make sure our pups are protected."

She reassured me with her smile and said, "Issa, I will be fine. And when you return in forty days, our pups will almost be ready to come. You have time to go."

I gulped back the tears at the thought of being a father.

She continued, "You must go when morning comes."

And at that, we curled up together and fell into a deep sleep.

*****

I woke before Romey did. I nuzzled her ear. She woke up and gave me a smile. I smiled back and nuzzled her one more time and then took off into the pre-dawn.

The clover was wet with dew and smelled of sweet honey. The early morning bees made a clearing for me as I ran towards the desert. The olive trees wished me well as I passed through their groves. The hummingbirds and doves chirped with me until the crags in the rocks got rougher and the sun grew hotter. It was at that edge of pasture and wilderness that they bid me a good journey to find my master.

I was not sure where to begin my search. I decided to return to the spot where we had said goodbye the night before. From there, I put my nose to the sand and began my search.

By noon the sun was scorching overhead. I was feeling light-headed and my tongue felt like it was cracking inside my mouth. I decided to rest under a thorny old tree that bore no shade at all. *But at least it's a tree*, I thought. I dug into the sand until the desert earth felt cooler, and then I lay down.

I woke up with a start. My nostrils flared and my lips curled. A growl came from deep inside before I even had a chance to figure out why I was growling. It was a smell. It was a memory from a far off place. "What is that?" I asked myself aloud.

I turned around and could only see miles of desert and reddish cliffs in the distance. At that moment a desert whirlwind started up and went straight for the red cliffs. I was suddenly swept up in the whirlwind. Within a heartbeat, I was thrust into the eye of this desert storm. "Help!" I cried…."Help!"

Whop. The whirlwind dropped me at the foot of the cliffs.

I was dizzy. My nose had been scraped when the windstorm released me. I hadn't had a sip of water since I left Nazareth, and I felt that soon I should die without it. I licked the blood that dripped from my snout and it seemed to give me some strength. I cried out loud, knowing that my master would understand, "Master! Master! Please let me know where you are. Send word on the wind, or send word by the sand beetles. Send word to me and I will find you and protect you."

I sat as still as a mouse. I listened and nothing came. No word. No message. Just silence—deafening silence. Soon the night came and I drifted off to sleep and fitful dreams of Romey and her belly and me in the middle of nowhere, doing no good for anyone.

I woke up at sunrise with aching bones and a sense of panic. *I must find water or die.* I decided to scale the cliffs. *Maybe there will be a mountain oasis.* I climbed until I discovered some wild mountain goats that didn't seem pleased to see me. They scattered and ran. I yelled, "No wait, I am a kind dog, I will not hurt you!"

They had disappeared as fast as they had appeared. I crept slowly toward the patch of desert grass they had been eating. It looked pretty good, so I took a mouthful and began to chew.

"Stop eating our food you beast!" came a voice from behind a large red rock.

"Come out from behind the rock," I implored.

It answered, "No. You come here first."

I didn't feel like arguing so I agreed and walked toward the voice.

"Stop there. Don't come any further."

I stopped.

"What brings you here? You look like a city dog, not a desert fox or a wild hyena. Do you mean us harm?"

I answered, "No. I mean you no harm. I am looking for my master who is fasting and praying in the wilderness for forty days and forty nights. I must find him so I can protect him from all harm."

The leader of the mountain goats appeared from around the edge of the rock.

He asked me, "What does your master look like?"

I answered, "He is young and handsome. He is tall enough to be impressive, but not a giant. He walks with grace and loves all creatures. He sometimes has a halo of light over his head, and birds sing to him and insects chant his name in the hot sun. Owls hoot for him at night and the fiercest of all animals turn into warm honey in his presence."

I could have gone on, but the goat interrupted me, "Yes. We did see such a man come this way, but he climbed to the very top of our mountain."

"I must go to him, but I cannot climb without water to drink, I am too weak to go on."

The older goat just said, "Harrumph."

I shot him a pitiful look.

He said, "Well then, come with me."

I followed the goat and he led me to a cave. I could hear the sound of dripping water from deep inside. The goat warned me to watch my footing, as the rocks were slippery. At long last, I saw a delicate waterfall delivering cold spring water into a pond. I looked at the old goat and he said, "Well, go on. What are you waiting for?"

I jumped into the pond and drank to my hearts content. After I satisfied myself, I thanked the old goat and was ready to climb the mountain and find my master.

The climb was arduous, but I finally reached the summit. I cried, "Master, Master can you hear me? Where are you? It's me, Issa!"

It was dead silent. I decided to run around to the other side of the summit, and to my eternal delight I saw him, my dear master, sitting quietly in the opening of another cave entrance. I ran to him and jumped in his lap.

He started laughing. "Issa, what are you doing here? How did you find me?" he asked.

I explained to him that I had come to protect him from all harm and that he had no need to be afraid of anything, now that I was with him.

He looked at me long and hard. Then he patted my head and rubbed my ears and exclaimed, "Oh Issa, you are a wonderful friend and one day you will be rewarded for your love and kindness."

I told him about my journey and about the old goat that led me to the spring water. As I was telling him my story, I began to notice that he looked thinner than the last time I had seen him. His cheeks were sunken and his lips looked parched.

I asked him, "Master is it alright if I leave for a short time to fetch you some water and maybe some wild honey and goat milk? You look hungry and thirsty, and it would be my great pleasure to do this for you."

He looked deeply into my eyes and told me that he was fasting and preparing for his return to Galilee.

And so it was that I stayed with him inside the cave for many days. He sat mainly and prayed out loud to his Heavenly Father, who I never met. I never saw this other father of his, or heard him speak, but my master prayed to him and listened to him in great earnest for many days.

Occasionally, my master would walk on the slopes of the mountain and enjoy the early morning air. I would just walk quietly beside him and keep him company.

Every afternoon, I would run down to the spring-fed pond inside the cave and drink as much water as I could, and then run back up to be by master's side. Sometimes the goats would leave me a bowl of milk or a scrap of cheese that one of the nearby shepherds had left behind. I was never gone long, and according to my calculations, it was the last week of his forty-day sojourn.

On the last night inside the cave, I woke up, greatly startled. My nose stung with an odor as rank as the devil himself. "Ahhh!" I screamed.

"That's him; that's the devil, I remember you!" I screamed again.

Sure enough, there he was, a shadow of a man, entering our cave. He was laughing and taunting me as he came closer.

I howled at him, "Owwwwwww. Owwwwww."

And then I charged the evil one. I pounced straight through him and then he was gone.

My master woke and asked me what was wrong.

I was afraid I had just dreamed about this evil man coming into our cave and I did not want my master to think I had gone off in the head, so I lied, "Nothing Master. I just had a bad dream, that's all." I hung my head because I hated to lie to my master, but I rationalized that I didn't want to worry him, since we had such a short time to go before we returned home.

I made my way to the cave entrance and plopped down, deciding to keep a safe guard. I had one eye going one way and one eye on my master. I noticed that my master looked very thin. I knew he was getting weak from lack of food.

I asked him, "Master, are you alright?"

He told me he was fine. He said, "My heavenly Father made part of me from Him and part of me from the earth. I feel the hunger today, that is all."

I wanted to leave and find him some food, but before I had a chance a most thunderous voice barreled into the cave. The voice said, "If thou truly be the Son of

God, you need but lift one of those stones at your feet, and say that it shall be bread."

I noticed the stones at my master's feet, and sure enough they even looked like loaves of bread. I wagged my tail, thinking that this would be a wonderful solution to my master's hunger.

But my master looked up and said to this voice, "It is written that man cannot live by bread alone, but shall be nourished in heart and mind by the word of God and belief in Him."

That is when the voice roared with disapproval and blew a tempest of sand into our cave. After the wild wind blew through with great force, the voice was gone.

Jesus was so weak from hunger and thirst that he sat down to rest. He hung his head and was soon asleep. I nuzzled close and realized he was feverish.
I tried to comfort him when he woke with a start and walked toward the edge of the cave entrance. He walked as close as he could to the edge of the mountain face. I joined him and looked down and got dizzy, just thinking about the fall. "Please don't stand so close to the edge master," I begged him.

He said, "I was dreaming Issa. Dreaming that I was on the uppermost part of the temple in Jerusalem, and I was falling."

At this point my master swayed forward and came alarming close to falling off the edge At the exact moment that my master swayed forward, the thunderous voice came back, but this time it was so powerful that the sky became black and it was accompanied by another violent wind.

The voice demanded, "Go on. Throw yourself down and prove to me that you are the Son of God; you know that angels will bear you up, you know that you cannot be dashed by the stones below. Go on, jump, I need proof."

My master stepped back and retorted, "Thou shalt not unduly call upon the power of the Lord thy God."

My master stood on the edge for a time while the wind thrashed and thunder struck. I trembled at his feet, not sure what to do. As quickly as the thunder began, it stopped. The sun came out from behind some clouds and he smiled at me.

We went back inside the cave and remained there until the next day, the last day of our mission.

I woke up that morning feeling very excited. I could not wait to go back home. "Master, it is time to go! Today is the fortieth day!" Then it hit me, like a falling tree…. "Master? Master, where are you?" I looked high and low. I looked everywhere. My master was gone.

I burst down the side of the mountain following his scent. I ran below the water cave and onto the farthest slope where a valley began. I saw him at last. I yelled as loud as I could, "Master, Master, wait up!"

He bent down to let me jump in his arms.

"Master, why did you leave me?"

He reassured me that he didn't leave me, that he was just on his way back up to tell me it was time to return home, to Nazareth.

I asked him what had happened that he ended up in the valley below.

He told me an amazing story as we struck back across the desert toward home. He said, "Issa, the voice came to me a third time, and I did not want you to be frightened again, so I asked the voice to follow me out to the valley."

I asked, "What did it have to say this time? "

Master smiled and he explained, "The voice offered to make me Supreme Ruler over all kingdoms on earth. He offered me a golden throne to sit on and he offered to place a crown of jewels on my head. He promised me every luxury known to man, greater than any king before me has ever had."

I was very excited, as I immediately saw myself and Romey and all our pups at the feet of our exalted master. All of us were sitting on velvet carpets and our pups drank from bowls that were made of pure gold.

I looked up expectantly to my master and that's when I knew that he could tell what I was thinking.

He looked down at me with a funny look on his face. He said, "Issa. Issa. You are imaging a grand palace made of gold and silver and you are seeing your family ruling the kingdom of dogs in Galilee, aren't you?"

I looked a bit sheepish and answered, "Well, a little bit, I guess."

He gave me smile and said nothing, but he touched my head tenderly.

I could not help but ask him, "So, what did you tell the voice when he offered you all the finery and power in the world?"

He replied, "I told the evil one, 'Thou shalt worship the Lord thy God, and Him alone shalt thou serve.' "

I did not understand what he meant at that moment, but I understood it some weeks later when were back in Nazareth and Romey had our pups. It was then that I figured out that all the gold in the world could not replace the love I had for Romey and for my pups, which I figured were a gift from above.

My master and I rested for several weeks upon our return from the wilderness. I was busy helping Romey with the pups and my master was helping us too. He loved the little ones and we would play together and have great times.

Fresh with the memory of our day's in the wilderness, I was not exactly excited when I saw my master walking toward the Jordon where we had met up with John the Baptist some months earlier.

As I watched and wondered why he was headed in that direction, I could not remain behind. I had to follow him and watch over him, for this was my responsibility.

We arrived at the Jordon and when the Baptist saw us, he began to hail my master, the Messiah. There were five men with John the Baptist that day and when they looked in my master's eyes they fell to their knees and worshipped him. They looked up and called him: "Master."

I started barking. *No,* I thought, *he is not your master; he is my master!* I was ready to defend my territory when John the Baptist emptied a wooden vessel filled with water from the Jordon River right on top of my head. When I shook myself free of the water I looked up and the five men and my master were laughing. They sat down and I went to them. I suddenly felt so happy and so in love with these men. I felt that I knew them and that they were now my brothers.

John the Baptist was laughing too. He said to my master, "Issa's conversion will be your first miracle."

I wasn't sure what that meant, but I didn't care. All five men introduced themselves to me. And by name they were Simon Peter, Andrew, John, Phillip, and Bartholomew. I got a surprise later that day when I learned that John the Baptist spoke the dog language just like my master and Sundar.

Later that evening as we were resting by the river and eating fish and bread, John the Baptist told me that these men were to be known as my master's disciples, and that it was their calling to listen to all that my master would teach them. And then one day they would spread His word to all of the world.

I didn't understand what he meant. I felt a shudder of fear go through me, and I didn't understand that either. There were many things, by now, that I didn't understand —all I knew was that I would stand beside my master until the end of the world.

CHAPTER 7

"People say he is the Messiah," Romey said to me late one afternoon.

I told her, "That is what John the Baptist called him." I reluctantly admitted that I didn't know what 'Messiah' meant.

She also said, "The rabbi and the people ask, 'Isn't he a carpenters son?', or isn't he just the son of Mary and Joseph? How can he be so learned?"

Romey and I thought this was rude, but my master never let this kind of talk bother him. Even Bartholomew teased my master about it and said, "Can any good come from Nazareth?"

But my master agreed with Bartholomew, and said, "A man can never be a prophet in his own town."

I wasn't sure what that meant either, but I do know that we spent less and less time in Nazareth.

One of the first official duties the six of us did with my master was to go to a wedding in Cana. Mary was helping to prepare the feast when we arrived. My master was an invited guest, but the rest of us came uninvited by the host.

I was sitting right underneath Mary's feet when I heard her say to my master in a whisper, "I'm afraid there

139

will not be enough wine for all the guests and the men you brought."

I followed my master out into the stone courtyard. He sat on a bench and began to talk very quietly. Naturally I assumed he was talking to me, so I listened carefully to what he was saying. He was wrestling with his soul. He wanted to use his power, but was unsure if it was the right thing to do. Then, out of the blue, he suddenly stood up and said, "Issa, would you bring the guests out here, and gather the five as well? "

I ran into the main room and barked and not only got the attention of the five, but the wedding party followed me as well. My master asked his disciples to fill the empty water jugs with water. They filled them all to the brim.

After that, my master stood over the jugs of water and stared down into the water. I could hear the whisper of a breeze. Then the ground shook a little and one of the guests spoke out, "Look, he has changed the water to wine!"

The wedding party was in awe. Mary was in awe. Everyone was asking him how he did it. One man asked, "Where did you learn this magic?"

My master said, "It is not magic for a grape to turn to wine."

And the man replied, "But there were no grapes, only water!"

My master smiled and before he could respond, the guests were declaring that my master had performed a miracle: "This is a miracle! This is a miracle! He has changed the water to wine!"

Soon, everyone started drinking the wine, and before long they were having too much fun to remember the mystery of how my master had performed this miracle.

I was not as puzzled as everyone else seemed to be. I had lived with master my whole life. I remembered the miracles in India, and could still remember what it felt like for Jesus to make me float in the air. That same night, on our way back to Nazareth, master spoke to us and he said, "I have come not to call you out of the world, but to show you how to live more happily and pleasantly in the world."

We decided to stay the night in our favorite olive grove. My master wanted to pray by himself and told me to hang out with the men. They were still very excited about the miracle and took turns telling their own versions of the event. Finally, Simon Peter spoke up. He said, "During the transformation of the water to wine, I felt a great tingling sensation in my arms and I was graced with a vision of how our sweet master made this happen. "

John said, "Go on Simon Peter; tell us what you saw."

So Simon Peter went on and said, "Because he is the Son of God, he knows all the processes of Nature...." He paused and sat down right beside me and started petting my head. This made me start to feel very relaxed and happy. My eyelids were getting very droopy as he continued..., "So what I saw, as if in a vision, was a field of grape vine. And I saw the roots of the vines and I saw the sap supplying nourishment to the grapes, and I saw the grapes being squeezed and made into wine...." He paused and lifted me all the way onto his lap. "...Instantly, in a way unknown to men, and known only to Jesus and his Father, Jesus shortened this process..."

Unfortunately, I didn't hear the last thing Simon said, because I fell asleep in his warm lap.

In the morning, my master told us that it was his mission to be present for simple joys, like the wedding, as well as to share in their sorrows, but I didn't like thinking about the sorrows.

*****

Capernaum is a town north of Nazareth. It is right on the Sea of Galilee. Master decided to go there next and Mary and Romey came to stay with us for a time. We had plenty of fish to eat, and Mary baked fresh bread everyday. But the best part for me was that Romey came with Mary. Life was good. Mary had found good homes for all our pups, so Romey and I were very happy. I had all my friends and family with me, except for my good friends Briden, Mosey and Sundar. I missed them a lot and I knew that my master missed them as well. Sometimes, when I got my master all to myself, we would laugh and reminisce about our adventures in India.

Our stay in Capernaum was carefree. Everyday I would leap on the boat and help the men fish. Sometimes, my master would join us, but usually he would stay behind to meditate and pray. He spent a lot of time alone. Sometimes I would worry about him and jump off the boat and swim ashore. I was still haunted by the devil in the wilderness and reckoned he could find us here too.

One night, my master asked that we gather around. He spoke to us and said, "Tomorrow I am going to Jerusalem for Passover. I will go to the temple that I knew as a young boy. I am hoping you would like to join me."

"Yes, of course!" we all shouted.

He went on to tell us, "I am sure there is a better way to worship," he said.

"What do you mean master?" Simon Peter asked.

My master answered, "I believe the slaughtering of doves and lambs and other innocent animals is wrong. And to do this for the sacrifice of peoples' sins is also not right, so I hope to show the people that there is another way."

I approved of this idea whole-heartedly and started wagging my tail and jumping in the air.

Simon Peter spoke up again and said, "We will follow you Jesus wherever you lead us."

And so it was that we went to the temple for the Passover festival.

We went to the same temple where my master had taught the old rabbis when he was a little boy. I knew the story because I overheard Mary telling the story to her cousin Beth a long time ago.

She began her story with the long trip she and Joseph took to Jerusalem for Passover. Jesus was just a young boy, and naturally went along. They stayed in Jerusalem for the festival, and joined the caravan back to Nazareth when the holiday was over. In lament, she described discovering that their son was not with the returning caravan. They had accidentally left Jerusalem without their Jesus.

"We thought he was at the end of the caravan playing with a cousin or a friend, and when we finally realized he was not with us, we despaired and made our way back to Jerusalem."

"What happened next?" Beth asked.

Mary continued, "I was convinced he had been killed by thieves, and as much as Joseph tried to comfort me, I could find no comfort, at least not until we found my child," Mary continued. "And so it was that we finally made it back to the big temple in Jerusalem. We decided to ask some of the rabbis to help us. Suddenly, we heard a young boy preaching with a group of elders gathered around. To our dismay, we discovered that it was our son doing the preaching."

"And then what?" Beth asked.

"Our son was baffled why we were so upset. He asked us, 'Did you not know I would be in my father's house?'"

I always liked the Temple story, because it had a happy ending. Mary and Joseph found their son Jesus and they made it back to Nazareth safely.

So I was in a jubilant mood that morning. I was prancing ahead of my master as we turned a corner and entered one of the temple courtyards. The courtyard was lined with stalls and the moneychangers who were shouting and arguing, trying to outbid the person next to them. When we stepped into the courtyard no one even gave us a glance. Next thing I knew, my master picked up some rushes that were lying close to the entry of the courtyard. He began swishing the rushes at the moneychangers and yelling for them to get out of his father's house. Then he raised his voice at them, "Depart from here. Do not stain my Father's house by making it a place for unholy bargaining!"

These men, who just moments before, were oblivious to us, looked into my master's eyes and obeyed him. No one seemed to even question his authority. They simply scrammed.

After that, more men joined us, twelve in all, thirteen including me. They had heard of my master and what happened in the temple.

One morning, all thirteen of us were on Simon Peter's boat. Master had been on shore meditating and we came back to join him. We were tired because we had been trying to catch some fish since dawn and had not caught one single fish. When we reached shore, my master told us to go out again. He said, "Go back out and let down your nets!"

So we did go back out, even though there was a lot of grumbling. Personally, I didn't care because I loved being on the boat. I loved feeling the waves bob me up and down and the wind in my face.

We didn't expect to catch any thing, but suddenly, I saw hundreds of fish and started barking. Simon Peter told the men to lower the nets and we caught more fish in that one moment, than we had ever caught before.

When we came back to the shore my master said, "From now on, I shall make you fishers of men."

After that day, we set out with a purpose. As I mentioned, there were thirteen of us. By name it was Simon Peter, Andrew, James, John, Philip, Bartholomew, Matthew, Thomas, James (we had two), Thaddeus, Simon, Judas Iscariot, and of course me.

More rumors were beginning to spread that Jesus was something more than just a prophet, or a scholar. Word had spread about the wedding miracle, and the temple. We began to draw crowds wherever we went.

"Everyone loves my master," I told Romey.

She cautioned me, "No, Issa, don't be fooled. There are some people who don't think so kindly of him."

This was the only time I can remember getting angry at Romey, but as the months went by, I could see evidence, that what she said was true.

I had no time to worry about these people who had problems with my master. We were too busy. Almost everyday, during this time, I witnessed a miracle. One day, I was sitting waiting for my master outside the synagogue and this old man kept talking to me in a gibberish that even I could not make sense of. He kept thinking that I had a turban on my head, and kept pointing at me and making a spectacle. This old man looked like he hadn't had a bath in years and he had seashells tied into his long beard.

He was screaming at me, "Take off your hat! You're in the temple!"

I couldn't say anything to him, because I knew that he did not understand dog. I also felt that if I started barking my head off at him, it would cause a ruckus and that would make some of the Roman guards come sniffing around. I put my paws over my head, but the old man was yelling at me so loud it didn't help.

To top it off, when he screamed, his seashells would rattle, so the commotion began to create a small crowd of onlookers.

One woman was laughing and said, "Look it is the mad man Lucas! He thinks that dog has a turban on his head!" That comment made everyone in the small crowd start laughing and pointing at the two of us.

A young boy said, "Lucas has been crazy since I was born. He sees things that nobody else can see!"

When the old man Lucas heard the young boy say that, he fell down on his knees and started pulling at his hair and pulling at the seashells in his beard. He was crying and beating the ground saying, "Why me? Why must I be so cursed?"

The woman that started the heckling screamed back, "You are not fit to be near the temple! You are filled with unclean spirits!" She picked up a rock and before she had a chance to hurl it at the old man, a hand stopped her.

It was my master!

The old man Lucas looked up and said, "I know who you are. You are the Holy One of God!"

My master walked up to him and put his hand on his head and shouted, "Come out unclean spirits!"

Lucas sat down and his head shook. He got up and said, "I am free. They are gone."

Matthew asked him, "How do you know they are gone?"

And Lucas replied, "For thirty years I have had a crowd of voices living in my head, all of them speaking at the same time. For thirty years I have had a crowd of eyes having me see a thousand different things at once. Never in thirty years has my head been still." He stopped and felt the seashells in his beard. He went on, "My head is quiet. There are no voices. The only eyes I am seeing from are my own." He knelt down and began to cry.

I approached him, still not sure if he would see the turban on my head. I nuzzled against him. He looked right at me and smiled. Then he petted my head and said, "You are a fine dog, and this is a fine day. I must go bathe and trim my beard, these seashells make me smell of the sea."

He did smell on the fishy side. I wagged my tail and the crowd marveled at the transformation. The young boy took his hand and said, "Let me take you to the well. You can wash there."

And so it was that the old man Lucas and the young boy from the crowd walked away hand-in-hand.

After people had heard about Lucas being cured of his madness, and how the unclean spirits had obeyed my master, there wasn't a day that went by that we weren't asked to perform some healing miracle.

We had a rich man approach us one day. He was distraught and begged my master to come home with him and heal his son. My master said to him, "Only when you see wonderful signs of my power, do you believe. You should believe without these things."

I didn't think my master had the time for the rich man because there were so many poor people who needed help and couldn't afford physicians, but my master looked at the rich man and said, "Go home. Your son lives."

I decided to follow the rich man home. I tiptoed behind him and when he neared his house, his servants came running out. They were saying: "He is well. He is well. Your son is well."

The rich man ran inside, and I overheard the man telling the servants about the man that told him his son would live. He said, "The man named Jesus. He is the one who healed my son, and he didn't even have to touch him."

When I heard him say that I barked and the rich man noticed me. He said, "That dog, he was with him."

I barked again and expressed my good day to him and took off. I ran back to my master and could not help but tell him how I followed the rich man, and what had happened.

My master asked, "Issa, did you not know it would be so? "

I said, "Oh no, I knew it would be so." But truth was, as many miracles as I witnessed, I still had doubts sometimes. I was not sure why I seemed to be cursed with doubt, but I was. I couldn't look back at Jesus right then, because I knew that he knew why I had to go back and see for myself.

There was another one of the thirteen that I knew had the curse of doubt and that was Thomas. And it was for this reason that he became my best friend out of the twelve. His best friend Bartholomew was just the opposite. The three of us spent quite a lot of time together. They could not speak dog, and they did not know that I understood them when I listened to them debate.

Bartholomew would say, "Thomas, it is so much easier not to doubt. Just tell your self that you have faith, and you will."

Thomas would say, "It's in my nature to doubt. I think I am stuck with it."

Then Bartholomew would say, "But you have seen the miracles."

Thomas would hang is head, in much the same manner as me. I would often think that he resembled a sad hound dog. "I wish I was more like you Bartholomew."

And with that they would go on with their business and I would Be left wondering if it was my nature to doubt, just like Thomas.

Our doubting was a quiet thing that we did not share with the others. And Thomas didn't even know that I was in the same boat as he. The doubting didn't affect the dedication, because there was not one among us who understood what was happening, except maybe Simon Peter, but because my master was so filled with joy and kindness, he didn't have to make miracles for us to love him. We just loved him.

And so it was that even a Roman Centurion heard about my master, and begged Jesus to heal his servant. This was a big deal because the Romans were becoming more and more a problem for us. My master did not have it in his heart to refuse anyone who needed his help. So my master cured his servant. I later found out that the centurion's name was Paul.

Our mission could have gone on endlessly. We could have lived forever helping the lame to walk and the blind to see. These were almost every day occurrences for us, but we had a few things happen that seemed to change our course. Namely, my master broke the Hebrew law.

The first law he broke was when he healed a lame man on the Sabbath.

We were just passing by the pool of Bethesda, in Jerusalem. This pool had been famous, for as long as I could remember, for having healing properties. The story about Bethesda was that every morning the spring would bubble for a very short time, and that in order to be healed, you had to be the first one to drink of the bubbles. So every morning there was a race to be the first one.

We were there bright and early on this particular morning, and I noticed a lame man, trying to crawl to the spring. I began to bark, and Jesus took notice of him. Lots of healthier people were crowding him out and making it impossible for him to make it to the well. So Jesus said to him, "Rise, take up your bed, and walk."

In the wink of any eye, the lame man got up and picked up his bed and carried it away as Jesus had commanded.

The crowd around the pool couldn't believe their eyes, and so master went into a shady grove after that to visit with the people.

I heard a whistle and it was Thomas asking me to come along with him to visit a friend who worked in the sheep market close by. We turned the corner and heard the lame man that Jesus had just healed proclaiming to some people, "I had been lying at Bethesda for twelve years, trapped and lame. The Nazarene, named Jesus, commanded me to take up my bed and walk, and now look at me!" He began to do a little jig of sorts.

There were some scribes nearby who overheard the man. They butted forward and asked the man: "When? When did the Nazarene command you to walk?"

"Today brothers, just now at the Bethesda Pool!" And then he did more dancing and hooting.

Thomas and I saw all this and knew the scribes were not going to take this lying down. Instead of visiting the friend, we went back to find our master, but he had left the shady grove. They told us. "He has gone to the temple."

Thomas and I were too late. By the time we got there, the scribes were charging our master with going against the Law of their faith. They were saying to my master: "How dare you break the rules! You are acting like you are God Himself. You are doing what is only reserved for God in Heaven to do on the Sabbath! What do you have to say for yourself?"

I wanted my master to play it clever, maybe apologize to the zealots. But before I had a chance to jump in and cause some kind of commotion, my master spoke up. He said to them," My Father works on the Sabbath, and so do I."

I put my paws on my head and looked up to Thomas who was biting his lip.

We got away that day with a slap on the wrist, but there was evidence that some of the people in town were not believers and thought my master was a disturbing influence in the land.

Shortly after that, we left the area of Jerusalem and headed north towards Nazareth. We set up camp near the base of a mountain right next to the Sea of Galilee. That night, the moon was just a sliver so the stars seemed exceptionally bright.

I was on the verge of sleep when a familiar voice called my name, "Issa. Issa. Wake up Issa."

I shook my head and opened my eyes to find myself looking straight at Sundar. "Sundar!" I was so excited. I instantly started barking, and naturally, when I started barking, all the twelve disciples harped back. "Hush Issa! We are trying to sleep Issa!"

Thomas even tossed his sandal in my direction.

I said to him, "They are a cranky lot."

Sundar thought that was funny, but immediately I could see that he was troubled. My stomach went into a knot. "What Sundar, what is wrong?" I asked. Mostly, I didn't want to know, because I was afraid of what he was going to tell me.

He said with tears of great sorrow, "It is Briden dear Issa."

"What? What about him?" I asked.

Sundar said very simply that Briden was very ill and that if I wanted to see him for the last time I must come now.

I didn't ask any questions. I didn't even think to look around and wonder what to do. I just took off into the night with Sundar by my side.

When we reached Briden, it was still the middle of the night. It was dark and the only sound I heard was that of Mosey braying. I ran to where I heard the dreadful brays and then I saw him. My dearest friend was lying still, with not a stitch of air rising or falling in his body. I went to him. I was so close I could smell the desert wind in his fur and the sweet musk of jasmine on the tassel that hung from his neck. It was the very same tassel that Romey had given to me so many years earlier. It was the same tassel that led me to my master when I was lost and near death's door myself. I then howled and sunk into despair.

Sundar was trying to blow air into his mouth, but Briden's beautiful jaw was clamped shut. I rubbed up to his belly and curled up next to him until I noticed the great Briden turning cold and stiff. Then I could hear Sundar comforting Mosey.

I wailed and I howled when from behind me I heard the voice, "Do not weep."

I spun around and saw my master. He was standing behind me.

Then he said, "I command you. Arise and live."

And at that, I heard a flap from Briden's lips. Then I heard another flap, and suddenly, Briden hoisted himself up, like a hornet had stung him on the backside.

He stood so tall over us he was looking down. "What? What are the stares for?"

Sundar was the one that spoke, "We thought we had lost you dear Briden."

The three of us were speechless. I had seen healing from my master, but I had never seen the dead brought back. I turned to thank my master, but he was nowhere in any direction.

Sundar told me later that he had never thought the dead could come back.

He said, "It is true. God has come among his people...."

Then he added, "...and his beasts."

I decided that night that I could never doubt again. Not after my master had spared my best friend. I stayed with the three of them for several days until I convinced them all to come back with me and meet the twelve men who had joined up with my master. "They are called disciples," I said to Sundar.

He said, "We were the very first, weren't we Issa?"

" Yes. We were the first," I said.

And at that, we hopped on Briden's back and set off for camp. Mosey trotted alongside happy as could be that her protector, Briden, had been saved. When the four of us arrived, we were astonished. There had to have been a thousand people surrounding the base of our mountain camp.

The multitude of people was looking at the top of a mount that overlooked the valley next to the Sea of Galilee. My master was speaking, and his voice could be heard perfectly. He wasn't yelling or speaking through a horn, but he sounded crystal clear and loud enough for all to hear.

By the time we found a spot to listen, my master was saying, "Blessed are those among you who are not proud, for you shall enter the Kingdom of Heaven... Blessed are those who mourn, for they shall be comforted...Blessed are the meek, for they shall inherit the earth...Blessed are those who strive for righteousness, for they shall be rewarded...Blessed are the merciful, for they shall be given mercy...Blessed are the pure in heart, for they shall see God...Blessed are those that make peace, for they shall be called the children of God...Blessed are those who undergo hardships for the sake of righteousness, for theirs is the Kingdom of Heaven."

I noticed Mosey had fallen asleep, so I gave her ear a nibble. She woke up with a start. Poor Mosey, I thought, *she doesn't have the kind of mind that Briden and I possess.* And as for Sundar, he was sitting cross-legged though out my master's discourse, and when it came to the part of Blessed are the meek, he started levitating. His eyes were closed and he was floating about six inches off the ground. No body noticed Sundar floating because everyone there was enraptured with what my master was saying.

After that day, more and more people came around to my master's way of thinking. His message was the message of love and peace. And the people seemed to like this message. But most important to this part of my story, is that after the big sermon in Galilee, Briden and Mosey and Sundar joined us at our camp, and they told the twelve how my master had brought Briden back to life the night before.

Thomas said, "But he was here the whole night. I know he didn't leave."

So naturally Sundar spoke up and said, "I beg your pardon, but I saw the master with my own eyes."

This went back and forth, until it was beat to the ground. We didn't want to bother my master as he was resting, so we decided that Jesus probably had the ability to be in two places at once. I was comfortable with this, and so were Briden and Sundar, but somehow I could not be sure how Thomas swallowed this theory.

In any case, Briden told me later that very early the next morning he thanked my master for sparing his life, and that my master simply petted his nose and said, "It was my pleasure dear Briden."

Well, that was enough for me. It was settled.

We had traveled by now, all over the region, from Samaria back to Galilee and all points in between. My master was practically famous and people constantly sought us out. They either wanted to be healed or wanted a friend or brother or sister to be healed. We even went places and raised the dead, just like my master did with Briden. My master never refused any one.

I suffer now, as I recall how I saw my master suffer such great sorrows. It took all his energy to heal, and he told me once that everyone's sorrow was his sorrow. That is why, when we got news of John the Baptist being thrown in jail, my master was most concerned.

Two men that were disciples of John the Baptist came to our camp with the news. One of them said to my master, "John has been accused of preaching against the ruler of the land." Then they asked my master, "Are you *He* Who was to come among us? Or should we look for another? "

My master asked them to remain with us for the day. They did and watched as Jesus healed many sick and made the blind see, and spoke the sweetest words of comfort to any one who was unhappy. So at the end of that day, my master turned to them. I was worried just to look at him, because he himself looked so tired. I could see that he was most concerned about the fate of John.

He asked the men to go to John, and he said, "Tell John the things you have seen. Tell them how the blind receive their sight again, and how the lame walk again, and how the lepers are made clean again, and how the deaf hear again, and how the dead are raised up into new life. And tell him that the Gospel is now being preached to the poor."

He asked that I go with these two men to deliver this message to John. He instructed the men, "If there is a message for me, please send it back with Issa, my dog."

I learned by listening to the two men, that John had been moved to the Castle of Macherus, east of the Dead Sea. Herod the King was staying there, and some dungeons near by held John in shackles. When we arrived at the castle, the two men told me to wait while they delivered the message to John.

They felt that they could have a better chance of slipping in without a dog, because the guard loved cats and two or three of these cats kept watch as well.

I was tired anyway and felt that perhaps just a short rest would set me just right. I lay on a patch of soft moss that provided me with a bird's eye view into the courtyard.

Inside the courtyard was a very large throne that was made from gold and rubies. Carpets and giant pillows were all over the marble floors and a center fountain sparkled with fresh water. There were bowls of fruits and stacks of flat bread and platters of goat meat and olives on a center table made from malachite. The goat meat smelled most delicious and it only reminded me of how hungry I was. There was no one around, so I tip toed into the courtyard and onwards towards the table. I looked both ways and grabbed what I could of the goat meat and hot bread. I then went underneath the table to enjoy my feast.

It was the best food I had eaten in months, maybe in my life. I finished and went for some more. No sooner did I grab another slab of the meat, when I heard clapping and bells ringing. From my perspective underneath the table, I saw a large man, draped in silk brocades enter the room. It occurred to me when this large man sat on the throne, that it might be Herod himself. Two women and several male servants were next to him, and within moments, ten or fifteen people entered the open room and began to serve themselves at the table. I was spared only because the table was covered with a beautiful piece of gauze fabric, the shade of a lavender bloom. I could see everything, but they could not see me.

A small group of minstrels started playing music and a beautiful girl entered the courtyard. She was, for a human, extremely pretty. She was draped in diaphanous scarves and wore a jewel in between her eyes. She had posed herself at the top of a marble staircase, and she indicated to the minstrels to start playing a very fast tempo dance. She started dancing. She undulated and crawled on her belly, she wiggled her bottom at the man on the throne, until he drooled. She was twirling in circles so fast, I felt dizzy. The small crowd was clapping faster and faster, until at last, she collapsed in front of the fountain.

She raised her head and spoke. She said, "And did my dance please you, dear Herod?"

He was breathing practically as hard as she was. He said, "Oh my dear Salome, you have moved me beyond measure."

Then she said, "I aim to please you dear king, but if I brought you such pleasure, is it fair that I may ask a favor?"

Herod said, "Anything you want my princess. Just ask and it shall be yours."

It was then that she said, "I want the head of John the Baptist. That is what I want!"

The room let out a collective gasp.

I could not believe my ears. *Surely the king would deny this insane request.*

I saw him hang his head, and ask her, "Surely, you would rather some gold, or jewels, or maybe a tower built in your honor? Surely, the head of the Baptist will not make you happy?"

All eyes were on Salome, including my own. She slithered toward Herod and looked back at her audience, and said, "It is only the Baptist's head that will make me happy."

Then Herod whispered into the ears of his servants and they vanished.

This is when I made my escape. I ran out of the courtyard and headed straight for the prison. I was running so fast I didn't notice passing the two disciples of John who I had traveled with. They started yelling at me, "Issa, come here! Where are you going?"

I turned around and started barking. They followed me and I headed straight for the dungeon. Just as we arrived, the two servants of Herod were dragging John the Baptist away in shackles. I was too late. The disciples had no idea at that point the fate of their teacher. They didn't speak the dog language so it did me no good to bark the message to them. Instead, I bolted and ran to John, despite the servants of the king. I could only say to him, "We will not forget you."

And John said to me, with great courage, "Tell Him I will see Him soon."

And with that, I ran back around to the courtyard. I was frantic. I was praying that my master would know what was happening by a message carried on the wind. I was convinced the savagery would be stopped, but in front of my eyes, it only took a second, a large Roman in a leather jacket, lobbed off John's head. He grabbed the head and placed it on a silver charger, and brought it to the Princess Salome. She was smiling, and some of his blood spilt on her scarves. The blood was spilling all over the floor and then they dragged his body away.

By this time, the disciples of John found me and saw the mess of it. They fell down and beat their heads. There was nothing I could do for them in their state, so I took off on my own, back to where my master told me he would be.

The whole way back I felt as if I was living in a strange dream. I kept seeing the Baptist's head, dripping blood all over the Princess Salome. I kept thinking about her dance and how she had even vexed me for a moment. I thought about how I had stolen the meat from the table and how my master always told the people not to steal, and I wondered if that commandment applied to dogs.

I decided not to return to camp. I could not face my master. It was final. I was going to make a detour and go back to Nazareth with Romey and Mary. They would never know what I had done. I would just tell them that my bad leg had started acting up and I was too tired to go on. They would understand and pamper me, and besides, I would have time to visit my dog children.

Then I found myself getting angry with my master. "How could he have let this happen to John?" I asked myself that question out loud, over and over again. Just when I was changing directions, and heading straight for Nazareth, I heard a voice, and a bright light shone down on my head. It called my name: "Issa."

I looked up toward the sky, for that is where the voice seemed to be coming from. My eyes were almost blinded from this light. I asked, "Who is it that calls my name?"

And the voice said, "It is me Elijah, once known as John the Baptist."

I screamed, "But you are dead. I saw your bloody head. You are dead."

And the voice said, "What happened to me, had to happen, to fulfill the prophecies. It was God's will, and nothing can stop the Will of God, Issa."

I confessed to him my sins and my agony.

And he said," Return to Jesus and tell him to go with John and James and Simon Peter to Mount Hermon. "

I was defiant. I told him, "I cannot face my master."

And he said, "Issa, we are made of flesh and bone, and we sin, that is what we do."

I remembered what my master said to a sinner once. He said, "Go and sin no more."

I decided I would return, but my heart was still heavy, and so I set out for the area around Mount Hermon, where my master was waiting for me, and word about the Baptist.

CHAPTER 8

The news of John the Baptist hit everyone very hard. I was the messenger and upon delivering the gruesome news felt as if I might as well have swung the ax. I stayed quiet and decided not to mention how I had slept on the job, stolen food and enjoyed Salome's erotic dance.

On the day that my master went up to Mount Hermon with Simon Peter, John and James, I decided to tag along. I had described to my master the strange vision on the way back to camp, and he was very intrigued that John had referred to himself as Elijah. He asked me, "Are you sure you heard the voice correctly, Issa?" I assured him that is exactly what I heard.

He then asked me, "Is there something else you want to say, Issa? You seem troubled."

I lied and said there was nothing the matter.

The trail up to Mount Hermon was craggy and rough. We were very tired when we reached the summit. Simon Peter and I lay down and were just going to rest for a minute. John and James followed suit and soon we were all fast asleep.

Suddenly, we woke with a shining brightness in our eyes. I immediately recognized it as the same light that I had seen on the road back to camp.

We adjusted our eyes, and there before us was our master completely transformed in a robe of bright white light that glistened like the sun. Then he raised his arm, and out of his hands came a flame, like when lightning strikes. Hovering next to him were two men, one on each side. They hung in the air, above the ground, as if they were certainly from Heaven and not from earth. Simon Peter recognized the men. He told us later, that one man was Moses and the other was Elijah.

Then a cloud came down over my master's head and a voice rang from the cloud. It said, "This is my beloved Son. I am well pleased with Him. Listen to His words."

My three companions on the summit fell to their knees and the voice then said, "Arise. Do not be afraid." Then we were instructed to not say anything about the vision.

The voice said, "Not until the Son of Man has risen from the dead."

As we made our way back down the mountain, my master told us that it was revealed to him that John the Baptist was Elijah the ancient prophet. He said to me, "I am sorry I doubted you Issa."

I assured him that it was fine.

We were still in awe over the spectacle that we had witnessed. None of us dared to imagine that our master would rise from the dead, because we never considered the possibility of him dying.

Later that evening I had my master all to myself. We slept next to one another, or at least I pretended to be asleep. I decided to tell him about what really happened at the castle the day that John was murdered. Since he was asleep, and not able to really hear me, I told him about the meat I stole; I told him about the flat breads I stole; I told him about the erotic dance of Salome, and how I had really enjoyed it; I told him about how I rested while the two disciples delivered the message. I did not leave out a single detail.

Despite the fact that he had been sound asleep, I felt better. I finally fell asleep with him that night, happy for the first time in many days.

*****

For the next five months we traveled constantly. Despite all the good that my master did, there were factions of people that were against us. When the scribes and elders found out about my master raising Lazarus from the dead, they were determined to put Lazarus back to death just to discredit my master. In their eyes, my master was a heretic. They thought he was undermining the faith of their temple, and that maybe he wanted to overthrow their government.

In truth, it was after the Baptist's murder, that things became more and more tense. As I have said, the elders in the church were getting nervous that my master was going to overthrow the old Hebrew laws, and the Romans were getting nervous that my master was gaining too much power.

We had more people join our inner circle. A woman named Magdalene had joined us, and a handful of the Baptist's disciples as well. Magdalene was very nice and rather pretty. My master liked her very much and I think some of the original twelve were jealous of her. I cannot say that for sure, but I know I was jealous, so I can only imagine that they were too.

As it happened, Sundar went to Jerusalem to show his maps of the stars to some wise men. He was close to the temple and overheard some Pharisees talking against my master: "The Nazarene is talking blasphemy. He is tricking these poor uneducated people!"

Another Pharisee said, "This is what that trickster said to these poor dumb followers…" And then he repeated my master word for word, "…I am the Resurrection and the Life. He that believes in me, though he shall die, yet shall live. He that lives and believes in me shall never die."

Sundar said the group of Pharisees gasped out loud when the witness repeated my master's words. When

Sundar came to us, and told us what he had heard, we decided to pack up camp and go to Ephraim.

My master said, "My time has not yet come. "

These were terrible times. I lived in constant fear that something awful was going to happen. We had received word that my master had been condemned to death by the Sanhedrin, the official council of the Jews.

I was so protective of my master that I did not leave his side. How could I under these circumstances?

When the feast of Passover time came closer though, my master decided it was time to come out of our refuge. We begged my master to stay in safety for a while longer, until the storm blew over.

Despite our efforts to talk my master into skipping the festival of Passover this one time, he would not shake from his plan.

We took the longer and higher road to Jerusalem. Many pilgrims were making their way towards Jerusalem, coming from far and wide. I asked my master, "Master, why can't we go back to India with Sundar and Briden and Mosey? We could be safe, and we could have fun together, forever and ever." I begged, "Please Master, just consider the idea. After all, we are experienced travelers by now!"

My master said, "Issa, just stay close. You are my devoted animal and our business is here in Jerusalem."

" Yes master," I said. But I was feeling a dread…a dread that I couldn't talk to anyone about, not even Romey.

We stopped in Bethany on the way to Jerusalem. I got a thorn in my paw on the way, but because I knew where Martha and Mary lived with Lazarus, I told Thomas I would catch up with them. I had never been so bold as to ask my master to heal me, especially for such a minor incident as a thorn. I pulled the thorn out with my teeth and took off to catch up with the rest.

Before I got there, I noticed that two men were exchanging goods on the road. One of the men was Judas Iscariot who was one of the twelve. I was going to run toward him and travel the rest of the way with him, but I saw him reach into the disciple's purse and give this man a coin for some figs.

Judas was the caretaker of our money and he was responsible for our bank. At first I thought that he might be buying figs for the men, or maybe for Martha and Mary, for letting us stay in their home. But he sat down and ate all the figs by himself. The money he spent was money that the poor gave to us, to give again to the poor, or help us continue our goodwill and acts of mercy. And there he sat, fig juice running down his chin, hanging his tongue out and licking the sides of his face like a wild cat.

He called to me, "Issa, come here."

I didn't stop. I barked at him and ran ahead.

I could hear him calling my name, "Issa, you come here. I command you to come here!"

Then he started chasing me, and I thought he might hurt me, so I ran even faster.

By the time I got to Martha and Mary's' home, I was panting and my tongue was dry as a bone. Mary greeted me and set a bowl of fresh water out for me to drink. I took two seconds to lap up a drop or two and set out to find my master. When I saw him, I told him what I had seen, and that Judas was stealing money from the purse.

He calmed me down and told me he had known all along of Judas' thieving, and said it was best to keep the matter to myself. "Do I have your word Issa?"

I could not understand his reasoning, but I promised to keep the dark truth about Judas a secret.

That night, after we had supper, Mary got an alabaster box of spikenard down from a shelf in her house. She began to anoint my master's feet with the precious ointment. Soon her entire house was filled with the rare scent. I was sitting right there at my master's feet and became scarcely giddy with the heady stuff. I was happy to see my master relaxed and joyful for the first time in a very long time.

Suddenly, the scoundrel Judas walked into the room. He began to have a fit. He said to Mary, "To what purpose is this waste? "

I began to growl at him.

Master touched my ears, and I stopped growling.

Judas went on like a fool, "Why was this ointment not sold? The money could have been used for the poor."

I wanted to pounce on the hypocrite, but again my master touched my head, and I knew he was asking me to stay still.

So master said to Judas, "Why do you trouble Mary? Let her alone, for she has done something good. She prepares me for my burial."

I stood up and let out a whimper. I jumped in my master's lap. Then I decided that it was just a ruse to make Judas feel a fool. And so I convinced myself that it was pure theatre to disgrace Judas.

Then master said, "The poor you will always have with you. But you will not always have me."

Still convinced it was make believe, I was content to go along with the farce that my master had created for the sake of Judas seeing the wiles of his ways. Later that night my master asked if I would get Mosey for him.

"Why master?"

He said, "It is Mosey's time to carry me into Jerusalem."

So I went into the night and made it to Sundar's camp and told Mosey what master had said.

Briden stepped forward like a proud parent and said, "Mosey, this is the moment we have been waiting for. You will be known forever in the history books. It is written in the stars."

Mosey and I took off into the night and arrived just before daybreak.

Mosey was so excited. Briden had told Mosey her whole life that she was an animal of destiny, even though she didn't know what that meant. She said, "Briden told me, that I would be in the Holy books one day."

I asked her, "Did he say anything about me being in the Holy books Mosey?"

She said, "No Issa, I think I am the only one who they will write about."

So wanting to make sure the event took place seamlessly, I had Mosey ready for the march into Jerusalem.

*****

Mary Magdalene held Mosey's lead, and I trotted alongside. Jesus sat atop her back and Mosey behaved perfectly. She was humble yet regal, and she held her gait steady and strong despite the throngs that followed them. People had torn green branches from the palm trees that grew nearby; they were waving the palms and crying hosannas in tribute to my master.

I could see Briden and Sundar craning their necks to see Mosey with my master on her back. Sundar was waving at us, and my master waved back at Sundar. It was a very joyful day for all of us.

I was sure, after our triumphal march that we were going to, at last, be out of danger. The crowds loved my master and I was convinced that when the elders met him, they would fall back in love with him, as they did when Jesus was a child. It was hard to think too much about the elders on this day, because it was my duty to lead Mosey back to Briden and Sundar, and by the time the day was over, we all fell into a heavy sleep. I woke up early and made it back to my master for the second day of the festival.

*****

Jesus went to the temple and was questioned by some Pharisees that wanted to trip him up. They wanted him to admit that he had broken the Laws of Old. As they were walking through the courtyard of the temple, my master saw that the moneychangers were back.

He yelled at them and said, "You are hypocrites. You say one thing and do another. You pay your taxes to the temple, but you forget the poor. You choke at a tiny fly in your throat, and yet swallow a camel!"

I hate recalling the moment that my master called out to them. As sure as I am of anything, it was at that moment that I felt like my master sealed his fate. The vendors fled the courtyard, and this riled the elders even more that my master commanded such respect.

On the night of the feast night, I went into Jerusalem with Simon Peter and John. We met a man who carried a jug on his shoulder and we followed him to a dwelling, which is what Jesus had instructed us to do. The guest room this man had prepared for us was very nice with a long table and benches for the men to sit.

Thinking back, it was rather brazen of us to come so close to where all the trouble was brewing, but my master wanted us to have this dinner together.

My master arrived a little bit early to make sure the table was prepared. The table was set, with the unleavened bread, a large platter of roasted lamb shanks, a bowl of salted vegetables and a bowl of bitter herbs. It was all I could do not to grab one of the lamb shanks off the table. Master noticed that I was drooling, so he pulled off a piece of the lamb and gave me a bite. This reminded me of the meat I had stolen at the castle, on the day that John the Baptist was murdered. I looked up again at my master and he was smiling. He asked me, "Issa, how long has it been since you have had meat?"

"I can't really recall," I said.

179

"I see," he said.

By this time the disciples began to arrive, and I was glad that my master's attention was diverted. He did a peculiar thing. He got up and took a towel and a basin of water and placed them on the floor. Then he began to bathe the disciple's feet. This is normally a custom that is performed by the servants of the house. When it came Peter's turn to be washed, he drew his feet away, and said, "I should be washing your feet!"

My master said, "If you do not let me wash your feet, you will be taking yourself away from me."

Peter finally gave in and let my master wash his feet. I was right behind Peter and after my master finished with the twelve, I stuck my paws in the water. My master said, "Come here Issa, let me dry your paws."

I did, and it felt really nice to have my paws so clean.

The men began to eat and talk. I was under the table and made sure I was sitting underneath Thomas, because every so often I would see his hand come down toward me, and he would give me a nice succulent bite of lamb. I was concentrating so hard on Thomas' hand that I barely noticed what was happening above the table.

I was just about ready to see if Peter might find it in his heart to give me a bite, when I heard an audible gasp from above. I came out from underneath the table and couldn't believe my ears. My master, Jesus, was saying, "Yes, it is so. One of you who eats with me now will betray me."

All of the men started looking back and forth, and asking, "Lord is it I? Is it I?"

I saw John lean in to Jesus, and I heard what Jesus said to him. He said, "The one I pass the bread to is the one." Then my master dipped a piece of bread in the meat dish and got it all soggy with gravy.

My mouth was watering. And then I thought, *Oh, my, what if he passed it to me?* At which point I ducked under the table. But I heard who thanked my master for the special bite, and it was Judas Iscariot's voice.

I felt safe so I came out again. I was sitting at my master's side. All the disciples had asked my master if they would be the one to betray him, all but Judas.

Then Judas asked, "Master, is it I? "

And my master said, "You have spoken. What you have to do, go and do quickly."

Then Judas got up and ran out of the room.

After he left, my master gave me a sip of some wine and a bite of the matzo. He told us the bread was his body and the wine was his blood. He told us that when he was gone, this would be the way to remember him. I could not bear the idea of it. I could not bear to lose him. I would save him, if I had to dive into the depths of hell, I would save him. That was my thinking that night.

One of the last things he told us that night was, "Greater love hath no man than this, that he shall lay down his life for his friends. You are my friends. You have not chosen me, but I have chosen you."

Then he started praying out loud, but I couldn't tell you what he said. The men were sobbing and I was nuzzled up as close as I could get to my master. The lamps had all gone out, and it was dark in the room.

I whispered to him, "Master, I hope I can lay down my life for you."

He patted my head and picked me up and held me in his arms. This embrace lasted some time and we were both weeping. He set me down as he stood up. He asked us to follow him and he led us to the garden of Gethsemane, on the Mount of Olives. It was cool and there was a breeze that made the branches sway. I would not leave my master's side, but I must have fallen asleep, because when I woke up he was gone.

I sprang to my feet. I saw Judas. He was kissing my master on the cheek. I thought, at first, that he had come to ask forgiveness, but then it happened. The Roman Guards appeared from the darkness. I saw Peter grab a sword and he cut the ear of one of the soldiers. That was all I needed to see. I ran and jumped on the back of the other soldier and sunk my teeth into his leather jumper. I felt my teeth go through the leather and pierce his flesh.

My master shook me off the soldier's back and said to Peter, "Stop. Put your sword back. All that live by the sword shall perish by the sword. If I wished to be defended, do you not know that I could pray and my Father would send me twelve legions of angels? It is written that what is to be, must be. Put up your sword."

And then, my master turned to the soldier whose ear was bleeding, and said, "Let me just touch you."

The moment my master touched the guard, he was healed.

The rest of that night is a blur. I remember my master asked them who they were looking for, and they said, "Jesus of Nazareth."

My master said, "I am he, but let these others go free."

Then the Romans placed my master under arrest. Thomas picked me up in his arms. We went back to Bethany and tried to figure out what to do next. While the disciples counseled amongst themselves, they didn't notice that I slipped out. None of them could speak the dog language, so I knew I had to find Sundar and Briden. I ran until I caught a whiff of Briden, and when I found them, I collapsed at his hooves in despair.

Sundar was with me seconds later and I told the two of them what had happened. "Sundar, what can we do to save my master?" I cried.

He just mumbled, "Let me think. Let me think."

In the meantime, Briden said that we had to tell Mary and Magdalene, who were staying nearby. Sundar agreed and he went to tell them the news. We set out the next day for the city.

We heard that my master had been taken to the High Priest, Ciaphas, and that he had been sentenced to death. The next day he was to be taken to Pontius Pilate and the sentence would be handed down.

Sundar said, "Issa, we have a ray of hope. The governor, Pontius Pilate, is superstitious. And he believes that our master is something special."

I didn't care about any of it. I only wanted to be by my master's side. I asked Sundar where my master was being kept.

"You don't need to go Issa."

But I begged him, "Please tell me Sundar, for I will have let him down and this is his greatest hour of need."

Finally Sundar told me and I went to the dungeons and crept quietly until I found him, my master. He was bleeding. They had whipped his back like a beast. His face was stained with tears. I crawled as quietly as I knew how, and when the guards became bored with taunting him, I licked his face and promised I would not leave his side until I knew it was time.

He was so weak he could barely speak, but he looked at me and I knew he was pleased I was with him. I was his first disciple and I was ready to die with him if need be. It seemed that for a moment the guards were going to let him sleep, but this was not so. They yanked him up and were slapping him and laughing and calling him the King of the Jews. One of the guards twisted a thorn bush vine into the shape of a crown and sank it onto my master's head. That's when I lashed out and they kicked me and screamed at me, "How did you get here you mutt? You go, or we'll make supper out of you!"

They kicked me in my ribs and I yelped out in pain.

My master commanded that they leave me be, but this only made them taunt me more.

They said, "Maybe you're the King's dog? Does that make you a Prince?"

They were laughing and the tallest one reached out and grabbed me and sent me flying through the air.

I landed with a thud.

I ran back to the dungeon, but the guards were too busy to notice me. They were building the cross for my master's crucifixion.

I crawled to him. We were both too weak and tortured to speak, but we were together, and I made sure I nuzzled his cheek, because I knew this was a gesture of mine he always loved.

Then they took him away and made him carry the timber on his back.

I can only say, that I stayed with him every inch of his walk to Golgotha. I followed him over the stone streets, and up the stone steps, and I stayed with his mother Mary and Magdalene at the base of his cross. I heard him say to Mary, "Let John be your son."

Then I heard him say my name, so softly that it was but a whisper. He said, "Issa, dear Issa."

I spoke to him and said, "Please master, please take me with you. What will I do without you master?" I pleaded to him as I felt the blood from his battered body fall onto my head, and on to my back and my paws. "Please take me."

He was barely able to speak. But he did say to me, "I am always with you."

One of the Romans had pierced him in the side and this is the blood that fell down on us.

The guards were laughing and joking, "King of the Jews, look at you now. You could save others, but not yourself!"

Then I heard my master say, "Father they know not what they've done."

He breathed in once more, "Father, into Thy hands I give my spirit."

And that is the last thing I heard from him.

Then the sky went black and the heavens cracked open. The earth shook and great boulders around the site broke open. The wind blew so hard, Magdalene had to hold on to me so that I would not blow away.

The Roman soldiers were quaking with fear. One of the men fell to his knees and said, "We have killed the Son of God." And then he wept.

A man named Joseph of Arimethea led Mary, Magdalene, and me to the place where a tomb had been prepared. That is where they placed his body. A large boulder was rolled in front of the tomb. I did not move or eat or drink. No one could console me, and I could console no one. Magdalene and John cared for Mary, but I alone stayed outside the tomb where the boulder had been placed. I wished it had been me on the cross, and not him.

Magdalene came to me early the next morning after my master had died. She put some water on my nose. She tried to get me to drink. His blood was still caked in my fur. She tried to wash it off, but with what energy I had left in my body I growled at her. I didn't want his blood washed from me.

She said, "Issa, you must drink. You must go on living."

187

I wanted to tell her to please do me in. I wanted to be buried with him, with his very blood on my fur. I wanted to tell her that my life no longer had purpose. Even the love of Romey could not be kindled. I had died with my master on the cross pure and simple.

My bones ached and my anguish was inexhaustible. I saw John coming and he bent down and picked me up. It was sunset of the second day, and as weak as I was, I jumped out of his arms and lay back down. He must have understood because he sat beside me for a time, and petted my head. He was crying, and finally I put my head in his lap and we stayed that way 'til night fell.

*****

On the third morning, some women came to anoint my master's body and prepare for his burial. I was in a deep sleep when they woke me. At once we noticed that the huge boulder was rolled to one side.

The three of us moved cautiously into the tomb. There was a light so bright, we could hardly see for a moment. The light faded a bit and we looked for him. I sniffed the entire length and width of the place. He was gone. He was nowhere to be found. I was barking at the shroud that was left, when suddenly we heard a voice.

It said, "Do not be afraid. You have come to find Jesus of Nazareth, who was crucified. Why do you look for the living among the dead? He is risen. He is not here."

I was barking when I heard the voice.

One of the women said, "We must go back and tell the disciples what the voice said."

They ran, and I ran with them, and on the way we heard my master voice for the second time. His voice said, "Fear not, but go and tell all my followers to go into Galilee and they shall see me there."

And that is what we did.

My master's ghost stayed with us for many days. It was a mystical time. The twelve of us stayed together and my master would appear and even sup with us. He spoke and we listened. The only one who continued to despair was Thomas, so I chose to stay close to him. Despite my master's presence with us, I still grieved. I wanted him back in the flesh. I wanted to sit on his warm lap and have him pet my head.

Thomas was uncertain and wondered if we weren't all under some sort of spell, and if these apparitions weren't just something we conjured up, as our grief was so great. He reckoned that we had all gone mad.

One night, Thomas and I stayed in a small hovel close to camp. We settled in for the night, when suddenly the room lit up. I heard a voice and I smelled my dear master. I barked, and Thomas looked up. It was my master standing before us. His side was bleeding just as it had on the day of his crucifixion. We could see the wound and I recalled his agony all over again.

Thomas fell to the ground and said to my master, "It is you. Finally, I see; it is you." And then he wept.

My master swept down and lay next to me on the floor. He petted my head and held me in his lap. It was the same warm lap that it had always been before. He told us that night, "Thomas and Issa, it is right that you should travel far to the land of India, and spread the good news." Then he added, "Sundar and Briden know the way."

Then he paused and looked into my eyes. He said, "Issa, You have been my greatest friend and I will be with you always."

And so it was that some months later, Thomas, Sundar, Briden, Mosey, Romey and I made our way to India.

*****

That was so many years ago.

Everyone is gone now, except for Thomas, Sundar and me. We stay in a garden right next to the church that Thomas built.

In the garden are the graves of Mosey, Briden, and my Romey.

I could never figure out why I was the lucky one to be rescued by Him, but I was, and in my old age, I am very happy it was me, and not some other dog.

In Madras, which is where we settled, the evenings are cool and before the sunset is over, I lay on the steps of our church. On several occasions, when I can feel a breeze tickle my ears, and ruffle my fur, my master comes to visit. He sits on the steps and rubs my head. I have felt his warm hand on my back.

We have walked in the garden and visited the graves of our loved ones, and he has promised me that we will all be together again in the most beautiful garden imaginable. My tail wags at the thought of it, and then in a whisper, he is gone again. But he always comes back and I know I will be with him forever.

Epilogue

Issa's Gospel was found behind the altar in St. Thomas's Cathedral in Madras India in 2011. Found with the text, was this letter, also written in Sanskrit:

> *I faithfully transcribed Issa's story and put the papers in a vault behind the altar. I don't know if his story will ever be found, or even so, if anyone would ever take the word of a dog, but I saw most of it with my own eyes and verify it to be the truth.*
>
> *Sundar Krishna Vidnu*

Estimates are that the text, which was written in Sanskrit, must have been transcribed by a Hindu holy man approximately two thousand years ago, according to carbon testing of the paper and the ink used to transcribe it.

Acknowledgments

I want to start by thanking my good friend, Gene Menger, for being my main encourager.

I also want to thank Eileen Keller and Mike Rinehart for their support and suggestions.

Phillip Wade was a kind and gentle teacher during the creation of the cover art. I am most indebted to him for putting on the soundtrack of Three Penny Opera, with Marlene Dietrich as our background music, on a very cold January day as he encouraged each brush stroke.

I relied on the great editing talents of Mindy Reed, The Authors' Assistant to make things right.

Without the tenacious will of Laura Toups and her steadfast belief in this project, it's possible, that The Gospel According to Issa, would still be collecting dust.

I suppose that my curiosity about the life of Christ could be credited to some rogue gene that I inherited from a Catholic mother and a Church of Christ father. The mix of these two elements was one of oil and vinegar while growing up, but in the long run, this rogue gene has served me well and led me down many paths of spiritual intrigue. So thanks Mum and Dad. And thanks to my three older brothers, Robert, Dusty, Tom, and the biggest dog lover on planet earth, my twin sister, Jean Ann.

Author Biography

Joan Black was raised in Fort Worth, Texas and gives credit to her home town for not only shaping her early career in music, but her inspiration to begin her first

two novels, *Grid of Saints* and *Burning Monk*. Joan sang with an eight piece jazz band with fellow musicians she met at the University of North Texas and later established a voice over career in San Francisco and Los

Angeles. Joan lived in Los Angeles for sixteen years, but in 2007 moved to Austin Texas where she now lives with her wonderful cat, Rupert Augustine Black.

Author Biography